TonyInterruptor

TonyInterruptor

or

Blue Cheese Amphetamines

Nicola Barker

GRANTA

Granta Publications, 12 Addison Avenue, London W11 4QR
First published in Great Britain by Granta Books, 2025

A CIP catalogue record for this book
is available from the British Library.

1 3 5 7 9 10 8 6 4 2

ISBN 978 1 80351 254 9 (hardback)
ISBN 978 1 80351 393 5 (trade paperback)
ISBN 978 1 80351 255 6 (ebook)

Typeset in Garamond by M Rules
Printed and bound by CPI Group (UK) Ltd, Croydon, CR0 4YY

MIX
Paper | Supporting
responsible forestry
FSC® C013604
FSC www.fsc.org

The manufacturer's authorised representative in the EU for product safety is
Authorised Rep Compliance Ltd, 71 Lower Baggot Street, Dublin D02 P593, Ireland.
www.arccompliance.com

www.granta.com

For Sarah Hall, who taught me
how to hold things lightly

&

For Tom Parsons, who doesn't really
give a damn about Mark E Smith

‘When I was 18, the vision was to make music that didn’t exist, because everything else was so unsatisfactory.’

‘Blue cheese contains natural amphetamines. Why are students not informed about this?’

MARK E SMITH

FIRST PART:

UNSTABLE ELEMENTS

1

One day, he just stood up in the middle of a live music performance and said: 'Is this *honest*? Are we all being *honest* here?'

He pointed at Sasha Keyes, who had just begun what he (Sasha Keyes) felt to be a particularly devastating improvised trumpet solo, and added, almost pityingly: 'You, especially.'

The interruptor had a good voice, a strong voice. It was fundamentally classless but with the slightest suggestion of northern grit. It had a pleasing timbre: low, grave, sincere. And the line was delivered in such a way that it seemed at once spontaneous but considered, indignant but measured. It was heartfelt. There was … somehow or other, there was *soul*.

Many people couldn't (or didn't) hear what the interruptor was saying because they were so intent on the performance. His words were just so much *sound* to them. They had – for the most part – paid for their tickets, and while the tickets weren't expensive (as befits an improvisational jazz show in a moderately affluent southern English cathedral town), nor were they cheap. Insofar as value for money is relevant to Art, that audience – an attentive audience, a great audience – were determined to get it. They were focused (there may even have been a degree of breath-holding) and the overriding consensus was that they were all definitely getting bang for their bucks:

Effortless flair –
Deep concentration –
Implacable scowling –
Occasional nonchalance –
Undeniable finesse –
Subterranean grunting –
Utter humourlessness –
Visible sweat –
Patent commitment –

Honest, though?

Honest?

Sasha Keyes was/is both a fantastically complex individual and an extraordinarily talented trumpet player. A virtuoso. That much, at least, is not up for debate. It's *known*.

*

Sasha Keyes was/is reputed to have once made Prince Charles cry after he slaughtered 'My Funny Valentine' (fearlessly, magnificently) while sailing down the Thames on a London barge. The (then) future monarch was held physically and aurally captive by this one-man last-minute booking and his legendarily uncompromising trumpet (Jamie Cullum had cancelled because of flu. The events organiser was summarily fired. This story may possibly be apocryphal, but it certainly rings true).

It also goes without saying (almost) that the gig wasn't much *fun*, but then who buys tickets for an improvised jazz set by Sasha Keyes and his Ensemble (the Ensemble didn't consider themselves to be 'his' or 'an ensemble' so much as a group of individuals who just happened to be playing together, several of whom actively despised each other) in the spurious belief that 'fun' would be involved? To expect (or require) 'fun' would be like going to a railway station (any railway station) and trying to book yourself onto a direct flight to Acapulco. This was an altogether different mode of transport. Fun was a point of neither departure nor arrival.

Over time, this moment – which we are now calling, for the sake of clarity, The First Interruption – would acquire a kind of mythical status. It became a little piece of Performance Lore; a source of ferocious interest/contention/amusement/debate across at least three creative disciplines, the subject of four books – this being the third – and the root of approximately 2.5 million tweets and countless memes. Even Sasha

Keyes himself would eventually come to see his involvement in The First Interruption as a marker of status (never a source of pride), although this uncomfortable accommodation was still a very long way off.

Very.

A very, very long way off.

And yet . . .

Even while we are calling it The First Interruption, can we be absolutely certain that this was indeed so? Was The First Interruption really the first interruption? Surely it must be highly likely that TonyInterruptor (John Lincoln Braithwaite to his mum and all the teachers who repeatedly threw him out of class) would have interrupted countless other live music performances, but that these interruptions had inexplicably (but also explicably) escaped public record? It *is* absolutely certain that he would've left many live music events in complete disgust, as such was his nature, and voting with your feet he considered a small yet revolutionary act of defiance (especially if the venue was seated and he was positioned, as he invariably was, dead centre, three rows from the front).

To stand, at a critical moment, during a live music performance – or a play, or a reading, or a maths class, or a poetry recital – and to leave (with all the adjacent kerfuffle . . . where's my anorak got to? Oops, I forgot my gloves) must surely be to surreptitiously disrupt and undermine a generalised feeling of consensus around what is 'good'?

For the record, The First Interruption wasn't especially notable or even outrageous (although some were outraged – Sasha Keyes in particular), but for a selection of obscure reasons it *became* significant. It represented a perfect storm. For a storm to be perfect there will always be a rare combination of meteorological factors (a serving of warm air from a low-pressure system hitting a portion of cool, dry air from a high-pressure system with a dash of tropical moisture thrown in like a condiment) which, just as in jazz improvisation, facilitate the creation of something potentially mind-boggling. Perhaps perfection is always a subtle and random amalgamation of disparate factors? Perhaps perfection is simply the unplanned conjoining (and unifying) of the unlikely? So brief! So fragile! (Sasha Keyes once keenly disputed this idea, out of sheer perversity, during a heated post-performance exchange with Fi Kinebuchi. We can imagine Kinebuchi making this perfectly sensible and uncontentious point in breathy undertones with her trademark flowery, birdlike gestures and Sasha Keyes gazing at her with an icy dismissiveness before saying something withering like, 'Have you thought about this a lot, Fi?')

In just this way (i.e. the perfect-storm way) there was the timing of the Interruption, the content of the Interruption, the general tone of the Interruption, the personality of TonyInterruptor himself (could we rightly call it charisma? This is a chapter in itself), the reaction of his interlocutor

(Sasha Keyes), the presence of a disgruntled Zoomer, India Shore, who had been compelled to attend the performance by her architecture professor father (Lambert Shore) in the belief that it would, at some level, be improving and educational for her.

Some people *thought* they heard what he was saying. Larry Frome (kicking butt on his ARP Pro Soloist 1975) was actually staring straight at TonyInterruptor, somewhat dazedly (and wondering how long Sasha Keyes would solo for this time around), when *he* heard the words:

'Sasha Keyes is a dick. A blowhard and a dick.'

This bears no resemblance to what TonyInterruptor actually uttered, but Larry Frome *to this very day* insists that it was so, even in the face of prodigious documentary evidence to the contrary (recorded on a mobile phone: #firstinterruption). This has opened up an entirely different area of enquiry #fromediffers around ideas connected to meaning and intent, and whether the human ear hears only what it *wants* to up to (approximately) 87% of the time.

It's interesting to wonder whether TonyInterruptor would even exist (as a meme, a metaphor, a celebrity, a concept) without Sasha Keyes – the very person whose sincerity he had pointedly and spontaneously called into question that particular night. Did Sasha Keyes actually *create* TonyInterruptor by sarcastically christening him, post-gig, with an idle, throwaway comment? Do we *all* inadvertently create our own mortal enemies by imagining them into being (and naming them), then spending inordinate – even heroic – amounts of energy fiercely battling with them through this crazy, mind-boggling delusion we call 'time'?

2

'A *dick*? Are you *sure*?'

Sasha Keyes is perched, uncomfortably, right on the edge, the lip, of the only comfortable chair provided in the small but nicely appointed artists' changing room. Larry Frome is keenly aware of this fact because he has lower-back issues and had assessed which chair might be best suited to his needs on first entering the changing room prior to soundcheck. Once this assessment had been made, he had allowed himself to believe that any other band member (they weren't a band, they were just random individuals 'performing' together) who sat in that particular chair and deprived him of it was a complete arsehole. Almost the entire band were arseholes, apparently; especially Sasha Keyes (who, in Larry Frome's view, behaved like an arsehole approximately 90% of the time).

Larry Frome is six foot three and incredibly thin. He is 47 years old and looks a little bit like Gil Scott-Heron. He enjoys wearing motorbike goggles even when he isn't on a motorbike (he once hired a dirt bike during a weekend on the Canary Isles in the early 2000s and stole the goggles – happily losing his deposit of 175 euros – because he liked the feeling of pressure around his eyes).

Larry Frome is celebrated for being extraordinarily frank and literal (he remains disappointed that he didn't see an actual canary on the Canary Isles, for example), but is generally liked among his peer group of musicians because he only ever speaks at a low whisper, which takes the edge off his caustic proclamations. Over time his trademark goggles (which have two tiny holes bored into the reinforced plastic on either side to preclude excessive quantities of condensation) have rubbed a kind of permanent parting onto the back of his head. His afro hair has formed into two distinct bubbles. It is a strange but good look.

Larry Frome suffers from ADHD and is incapable of sitting still for more than three minutes at a time unless he happens to be deeply engrossed in something. Generally the two things that engross him most deeply are vintage synths and arguments. He rarely eats, and finds swallowing difficult because he sometimes completely forgets how to do it properly unless he isn't concentrating.

'That's not even remotely close to what I heard,' Saul Timpson shrugs, distractedly removing one of Fi Kinebuchi's dark hairs from the arm of his new, bright yellow Crew jumper.

Saul Timpson always acts with a measure of grandiosity – as

if he were the rightful heir to the key-cutting, shoe-mending business Timpson's. But he isn't. He's just a 63-year-old geography professor from Reading with a talent for the cello who sometimes gets gigs with Sasha Keyes (whenever Cecil Home is busy) because his sister was Sasha Keyes's first ex-wife and he is a fat-headed but fundamentally amiable sycophant. He also holds an especially important place in Sasha Keyes's heart for introducing him (as a raw, unschooled 19-year-old) to Pharoah Sanders and – via Coltrane – the whole concept of 'sheets of sound'. Other ensemble members sometimes refer to Timpson, pityingly, as 'The Whipping Boy'.

'What did you hear, Tims?' Sasha Keyes demands.

'I heard "Is this *honest*? Are we being *honest* here? *You* especially."'

Tims points at Sasha Keyes. He holds out his pointing arm with a measure of Gothic aplomb, like the Grim Reaper.

'What the fuck? Some random fucking nobody,' Sasha snarls, 'some dick-weed, small-town TonyInterruptor . . .' He temporarily runs out of invective because his levels of upsetness are too profound to be fully encapsulated by mere words (or 'worms', as Larry Frome likes to refer to them – semi-seriously).

'TonyInterruptor,' Larry Frome echoes, 'one worm? Heh!'

'Surely the title of an early Fall single?' Simo Treen chuckles, also impressed, in spite of himself.

Simo Treen plays piano.

Simo Treen has been fascinated by the tonal peculiarities/sonic and compositional variations of birdsong *forever* – long before anyone else was even vaguely interested in the subject (although, to be frank, everyone has *always* been interested in the sonic and compositional variations of birdsong). Treen, who records everything, commences filming with his iPhone and deftly follows up his 'Fall' comment with the apparently unrelated observation that 'Sasha has never really had the capacity to fully galvanise a group of people.'

'What the hell?!' Sasha turns on him, outraged.

Never had the capacity to fully . . .?

This is precisely the kind of unnecessary sideswipe for which Simo Treen is legendary. He is a small but very muscular and hairy man with immense hands. He insists on always wearing shoes with impossibly pointed toes even though it must, inevitably, compromise his use of piano pedals. For this reason he has perfected a style of pedal-free piano playing. Nobody knows which came first – the pedals or the shoes. In-the-know contemporaries like to call this 'the Simo Treen shoe/pedal conundrum'.

'TonyInterruptor,' Fi Kinebuchi notes, thoughtfully. 'I expect you are familiar with the Krishnamurti quote that "when you teach a child that a bird is named 'bird' that child will never see a bird again"?'

'What the . . .? How the . . .? Shut the fuck up, Fi,' Sasha snaps. Fi's possession of a vagina makes her interjections, if possible, even more irritating to Sasha Keyes than Simo Treen's (and this is a proven, scientific fact).

'*You* shut up you *fucking dick*,' Larry Frome whispers, almost inaudibly, while fishing around inside his mouth for one of Fi Kinebuchi's hairs which he appears to have partially swallowed.

(Larry Frome and Fi Kinebuchi are currently an item although they live in different cities.)

'Krishna . . .?' Simo Treen echoes, 'What exactly has TonyInterruptor to do with birdsong again?'

Nobody can ever really tell whether Fi Kinebuchi is actually the profoundly mystical and otherworldly intellectual that she appears to be. She plays the autoharp and the lyre but also the guitar. She lectures in music at Christ Church University (several of her students were in attendance at the gig – Lambert Shore regularly corners her in the staffroom) and is generally known (by herself – on her social media – and therefore by the world at large) as 'The Queen of Strings'.

Some people (notably Sasha Keyes) think a) that she is the 'queen of strings' but the mistress of none, and b) that she just googles things and then randomly inserts them into conversations no matter how pertinent or relevant they may be. This means that she is invariably surrounded by a perplexing nimbus of question marks. She wears these like her queenly ermine. Sasha Keyes thinks she plays a devilish and cunning peek-a-boo within the voluptuous folds of this furry cloak.

Sasha Keyes was married to Fi Kinebuchi for seven years. For six of those years Fi Kinebuchi was living abroad and studying medicine, in Oslo. One month before taking her finals, Fi Kinebuchi abandoned her degree. Sasha Keyes found this impossible to comprehend at the time. He still hasn't forgiven her.

While we are on the subject of fur: if Fi Kinebuchi were to be said to resemble anything, then it would be an Alaskan Klee Kai. This is a relatively new toy breed of dog that (in turn) slightly resembles the Alaskan Malamute and the Siberian Husky and was recently popularised by the dog Nico in the American reality TV show *Couples Therapy*. The Klee Kai is adorable and dynamic and sheds its hair all year round. Fi Kinebuchi is tiny with a pointed face and bright blue eyes. She is adorable and dynamic and possesses a fabulous frizz of curly hair which *she* sheds all year round.

Saul Timpson (who is greatly enjoying his current role in the conversation as 'interpreter'/He Who Brings Clarity) says, 'When you name a thing you at once create *and* destroy it.'

Fi Kinebuchi turns to look at Tims with a measure of astonishment.

Did I really just say that?

How wonderful!

'Oh thanks for helping us all out there, Tims,' Sasha Keyes rolls his eyes (while simultaneously deciding if he agrees with this helpful précis or not. He doesn't because he refuses, on point of principle, to ever agree with any of Fi Kinebuchi's gnomic utterances.)

As Sasha speaks, Simo Treen is inspecting the venue's hashtag on his iPhone and noting that there is already a post on the stream in which TonyInterruptor can be seen (at a slightly unusual/unflattering angle) asking whether everyone is being honest. He immediately likes it and inserts the comment '#TonyInterruptor' to the feed then copies the post onto his Stories, adding the comment: #TonyInterruptor … heh heh WTF?!

He then starts a poll at the bottom of the post: Agree? Disagree? LET'S VOTE PEOPLE!

There is a gentle tapping on the small refreshments table which currently holds a selection of empty water bottles and crisp packets. It is Tod Knowles. Tod Knowles is a percussionist. He is tapping on the table with a plastic straw. Tod Knowles likes to announce every utterance he produces (he doesn't say much, otherwise this tendency might be extremely wearing) with a small, preliminary drumroll:

Ppprrrrrum-pum-pum pum!

'I dunno. Did I get this wrong or did this interruptor guy actually say that our music-making lacks integrity? Did I get this wrong? Because … yeah … that kinda *hurts* man. That stings.'

A short silence follows. It's almost as if nobody has considered this idea previously aside from Sasha Keyes, who took the whole thing as a personal (rather than a communal) insult. But yeah … now he comes to think of it … Sasha starts to smirk then stops smirking. *Does* this improve things for him, personally, though? Isn't it *always* better to just be slap-bang in the centre of attention (negative or positive)?

'I like to think that I'm an honest person,' Fi Kinebuchi muses, 'but in terms of performance …? Hmm.'

'Hmm?!' Sasha Keyes parrots, satirising her enragedly. (An 'honest' person?! Really?! Off being a mature student in Oslo for six years and then Oh sorry, I just don't think I actually want to do this after all . . .?

Total bollocks.)

Fi gently expands on her position: 'This was an improvised set, yes, absolutely, but surely we are all subject to various group dynamics which subconsciously – or consciously – underpin . . . Would you stop filming me, please, Simo? I actually find it a little bit disconcerting.'

'What I think Fi is attempting to say,' Saul Timpson delightedly returns to his 'interpreter' role, 'is that we all operate within a certain unstated understanding of who does what, when and for how long. A kind of unspoken contract, I suppose . . .'

'Does he have an "off" button?' Larry Frome whispers.

'Does he have an "on" button?' Sasha Keyes counters (also at a whisper).

'I'm not entirely sure if that makes any sense,' Larry Frome responds.

Sasha Keyes rolls his eyes. These people are fools. A bunch of fools. He takes a quick swig of his beer.

'Did you brush your unruly fucking *mane* over this table earlier, Fi?' Sasha asks, pulling a long strand of said mane out of his beer glass. 'I thought we agreed you'd always tie it back in our communal spaces?'

'Oh fuck my head is going to explode,' Larry Frome sighs.

3

Lambert Shore is excitedly telling his wife, Mallory, about a brief conversation with TonyInterruptor which took place while queueing for their coats after the gig.

TonyInterruptor did not deign to introduce himself even though Lambert Shore had gently tapped his arm, held out his hand and said, 'Hi. I'm Lambert Shore. I'm an architecture professor at Christ Church University. My daughter . . .' he indicated, vaguely, over his shoulder towards India, who was casually knocking back the advances of a boy in the year above her at school, while also surreptitiously trying to persuade him into selling her his old vape (which happened to be a punchbox unregulated parallel handmade box mod from True Mods. This vape was made in 2015 which to India – who was made in 2007 – rendered it impossibly desirable and antique) . . .

'Um . . . yes . . . that's my daughter. She actually filmed the comments you made earlier – entirely by accident – on her iPhone and posted them onto her social media . . .'

TonyInterruptor gazed at Lambert Shore, then peered over at India Shore, then glanced back at Lambert Shore, blankly, as if he had entirely forgotten about said 'comments'.

'Okay,' he murmured, after a couple of beats.

'Are you local?' Lambert Shore wondered, still holding out his hand.

'Uh, you'd probably need to define your terms . . .' TonyInterruptor frowned (as if agreeing to the requirements of a concept as broad as 'local' would involve more fudging and compromise than he could comfortably tolerate during a brief conversational exchange).

After what felt like an inordinately long interval, TonyInterruptor took Lambert Shore's hand and shook it, wearing an expression of gentle bemusement (to *shake someone's hand*? Seriously?! I mean what better demonstration of white supremacy/capitalist grind than this smallest of formal gestures?)

'I object to handshaking on ideological grounds,' he confessed, 'but you seem well-meaning so I'm happy to respond in the vernacular you're most comfortable with.'

'I object to handshakes on *ideological* . . .?!' Mallory parrots, astonished, 'Are you serious?'

'His exact words,' Lambert nods, gravely.

'Why would you object to a *handshake* of all things?' Mallory demands (although Mallory habitually approves of – and objects to – pretty much everything in her life with equivalently rigorous levels of vigour).

'I know literally nothing about the history of hand-shaking,' Lambert confesses, somewhat forlornly, 'perhaps there's way more subliminal political meaning embedded in this everyday gesture than we realise – I dunno – like an unconscious allusion to something intrinsically fascistic . . .?'

'You have such an embarrassing *man-crush* on this lunatic!' Mallory guffaws. 'What did you say his name was again?'

'He didn't actually introduce himself.'

Lambert Shore is tight-lipped. He is wounded. Does Mallory *always* need to be so . . . so relentlessly sassy and unapologetically tart? So insufferably ebullient?

(The answer to this question – on purely empirical grounds – is a resounding YES. At one stage in their relationship these had been precisely the characteristics which had rendered her irresistible to him. She was just so . . . so marvellously *impossible*.)

'Huh? Why not?' Mallory persists (she always persists; like a seagull up to its knees in sea-swell, determinedly dissecting a crustacean as it rolls ceaselessly back and forth).

'I don't know. Careful? Private? Highly secretive? I don't know.'

'Cussed. Just plain cussed!' Mallory snorts.

'I was a total stranger approaching him at a gig . . .' Lambert shrugs.

'Paranoid. Obsessive. A complete egomaniac.'

'Um.'

Lambert Shore scratches his head.

'What does he look like?'

Lambert considers this question for a moment, 'Quite tall. Lean. A mix of Anders Danielsen Lie – the Norwegian actor – and . . .'

'I *know* who Anders Danielsen Lie is, Lambert!' Mallory exclaims. She is unloading the dishwasher and almost drops a mug in her irritation. 'Please don't treat me like one of your idiotic students!'

Lambert Shore opens and then closes his mouth.

(At one stage Mallory *was* one of his idiotic students.)

'The handshake?' Mallory demands. 'Weak? Flaccid?'

'Long.'

'Sorry?'

Mallory straightens up.

Lambert suspected TonyInterruptor might actually be an alien from another planet, but he nodded his head obligingly (the nod representing the registering of something essentially inexplicable yet nonetheless marvellously profound) before doggedly ploughing on, 'I was just fascinated to understand what you *meant* exactly when you called Sasha Keyes "dishonest", earlier . . .'

'Hmm . . .' TonyInterruptor simulated slight surprise at Lambert Shore's 'angle'.

'Might you release my hand now, perhaps?' Lambert Shore wondered.

'Oh . . . Okay. Yeah . . .' TonyInterruptor let go of Lambert Shore's hand (his excessive shaking had brought an almost farcical element to what was previously – in Lambert's mind, at least – a perfectly straightforward and amiable gesture of greeting).

TonyInterruptor inspected Lambert Shore intently. Lambert Shore was/is a small, slim, perfectly formed late-middle-aged man with a boyishly handsome face and a greying blond quiff. He always combines expensively tailored suit jackets with beautifully faded jeans and impeccably crafted trainers.

'I don't think I *did* call Sasha Keyes "dishonest",' TonyInterruptor reasoned, 'It wasn't an attack. I'm not in the business of attacking things – or people. I think I simply asked whether we were *all* being honest. It was a completely spontaneous enquiry about the true nature of improvisational performance, which I suppose became, in turn, almost *a part* of the performance, and so – at some level – the most authentic thing about it.'

TonyInterruptor started to pull on his jacket. He was plainly intent on leaving.

Lambert Shore (a man of considerable ego himself) silently pondered whether TonyInterruptor might be an egomaniac.

'Wow,' Mallory Shore interjects, 'The vanity of the man! Those are precisely the kind of pretentious comments *you* might be expected to make after a couple of drinks. Was he rat-arsed?'

Lambert ignores this. 'So then *I* said, "Is authenticity

intrinsically more important or interesting than musicianship in performance? Do the two things always necessarily need to co-exist?"'

'Haha. Oh you *were* pissed,' Mallory chuckles, drolly. 'How did he respond?'

'He said, "Yes," then immediately added, "Radiohead *slash* Muse ... although I don't have much time for either, as it happens ... the Beatles *slash* the Monkees. Truth is beauty." Then he laughed. Then he ruminated for a moment and said, "I feel like I aged approximately five years during the course of this conversation."
Then he walked off.'

Before he walked off, TonyInterruptor smiled. When TonyInterruptor smiles the sun comes out. He rarely smiles, except in triumph. Lambert Shore mentioned the laugh to Mallory but he didn't mention the smile (he was still smarting from the 'man-crush' comment), although he was completely dazzled by the openness of the smile and gazed up at TonyInterruptor in that moment with something amounting to awe.

This man *was* truth. This man *was* beauty.
I dunno. Kind of. Somehow.

'"Daydream Believer"!' Mallory squeaks, outraged (she is an ardent fan of the Monkees). 'How *dare* he?!'

'Yes.'

Lambert Shore shrugs. He knows (and indulges) Mallory's intense feelings about Michael Nesmith.

'"The true nature of improvisational performance . . .?"' Mallory Shore continues unloading the dishwasher, 'What does he mean by that, exactly?'

Mallory Shore is a trained barrister.

'I suspect he's calling into question whether most "improvisation" is truly spontaneous,' Lambert responds. 'He probably feels like it's generally just the rolling out of a series of familiar musical tropes – recurrent themes and motifs – and all dependent on various traditional ideas about *non*-traditional musical composition, as well as established power relationships in the group etc. But he was also saying that what *he* did – his interjection – *was* improvised, or truly spontaneous, and therefore honest.'

'And he couldn't just wait until *after* the performance to make that point, maybe quietly, to a friend?'

Mallory pauses. 'If he has any friends. Was he there with a friend?'

'He became a part of the performance. If improvisation actually means that a thing is truly unplanned and spontaneous, then surely . . .? Um. No. So far as I could tell he was attending the gig alone.'

'He's taking everything back to first principles when in actual fact there *are* no first principles . . .'

'Um. Very possibly.'

(Lambert Shore doesn't really know what Mallory Shore means.)

'I mean there's a *contract*,' she persists, 'an informal contract that if I pay money and buy a ticket to go and see a live music performance then I should expect to be able to watch that performance without another audience member unduly compromising it. You know, clambering onto the stage with a penny whistle and tooting along, singing loudly, clapping out of time at inappropriate moments ... That's the agreement. That's the contract. The venue promises to deliver the performance to me – whatever it may be, improvised or no – without interruption. I must also fulfil *my* part of the contract because otherwise I will get turfed out for compromising the performance for the rest of the audience who are *also* informally contracted to behave in a way that is conducive to the well-being of the whole ...'

Mallory Shore is not a practising barrister because she spends much of her time looking after her eight-year-old daughter, Gunn, who has special needs, and is also (like her mother) magnificently quarrelsome. When she gets the opportunity to work, Mallory is a superb legal copy-editor (on travel insurance documents, mortgages, etc.). She loves to submerge her ferocious intellect into astonishingly mundane levels of detail. There's almost a kind of mischief in it. To be so unrelentingly *precise* in the creation of something cast iron and unassailable.

Lambert Shore PhD stopped paying attention after 'that's the agreement'.

'Show me the thing on your phone,' Mallory demands, while simultaneously grabbing her own phone from the kitchen table and going to India's Instagram herself. India is not her biological daughter. Mallory would never have christened a child of hers with the name 'India'. The very thought is inconceivable to Mallory, who feels strongly about everything (including names).

Lambert Shore takes out his phone (nonetheless), finds the link to India's post on it, and then blinks at the number of likes. He notices Simo Treen's comment/hashtag.

'TonyInterruptor,' he marvels, 'Simo Treen *himself* has hashtagged him! That's hilarious.'

'TonyInterruptor? Sounds like the title of a Fall song,' Mallory muses. 'Good heavens! She's received over three *thousand* likes! Who even knew that Sasha Keyes – or Simo whats-his-name – had that level of pulling power?'

Lambert has now crossed over to Simo Treen's Instagram and sees *his* post.

'This thing is going viral!' he exclaims, 'There are already 418 comments. People are really engaging!'

'Talk about a storm in a fucking teacup,' Mallory clucks.

'I dunno. Is this good or bad?' Lambert wonders out loud. 'I can't decide.'

Is this good or bad?

Lambert Shore can't decide. He looks to Mallory for guidance. Mallory always knows what to think, thank God.

He suddenly notices India standing in the doorway, listening intently to their conversation. Her expression is inscrutable.

'Did you see this thing?' he asks, holding out his phone, 'It's blowing up, kiddo!'

'"Blowing up"?!' Mallory snorts.

'Is this *seriously* how normal people talk to each other in their kitchens?' India demands, aghast, 'Because if it is, I swear to God I may as well just end it all now. It feels like . . . I dunno . . . like being dead already. Like having your brain gradually syringed through your ear. Like . . . *urgh* . . . like being roasted alive in a firepit of stupid *blah blah blah*. Do the two of you ever say anything *real* to each other? Is anything ever actually *real* in this house?'

She pauses.

'Honest?' she rejigs, effortlessly. 'To be *honest*? With each other? With yourselves?! Do you even have any idea what that *means*?'

4

John Lincoln Braithwaite is real. When he cuts himself shaving he bleeds blood, not ideas. He does real stuff. He has real virtues, vile habits and serious aspirations.

He is a smoker. He is not a smoker because he needs to smoke, but because he senses, subconsciously, that the cigarette is one of the only remaining ways in which the modern human can sit or stand in space and be quietly permitted to inhale. Just to pause and inhale. A primordial punctuation. In the way that some ancient primate sits by the side of a dirt road and gently scratches itself and sniffs and evaluates its surroundings with a ruminative, speculative gaze. This is smoking for John Lincoln Braithwaite. A kind of permission. A quiet time. A tranquil time.

Smoking is a condensed and bastardised form of fire-watching. A meditation but without the portentousness of a meditation. It isn't idleness. It isn't gesture. It isn't defiance. It is stillness.

When John Lincoln Braithwaite smokes (or returns to his smoking place, his smoking mindset), his main occupation – his duty, even – is to observe and assesses the falling and the catching of light. This is his favourite pastime – a mental abstraction. He is profoundly moved and gratified by the light falling and glancing and flashing and refracting. There is nothing more immediate and seductive for him than this. A beautiful woman, a lovely song, a delicious meal ... these sensual delights pall by comparison with the play of the light, because the play of the light isn't considered, it's purely incidental. It requires no effort and no human intervention. It just is.

The light *will* fall. It will creep in, sneak in – persistently, doggedly, determinedly – come hell or high water. Sometimes it will charge in, at high speed, darting and slithering, skittering and flashing. Or it will lie passively in a misty pool, softly illuminating. Or it will bake and scorch; sharpening edges and hardening surfaces. It can be tiny. It can be immense. It can be every imaginable shape and some unimaginable. It can smash or shatter – like a mean silver hammer – or spread, honey-yellow-yolk-golden. It can glance and slant and shimmer, gently refracting, glimmer-blue-whitely. It can shout loudly. It can barely whimper.

The light will fall. Its empire is infinite. The whole earth is its palette, its plaything. Nothing is anything without light. The world is just so much hopeless tripping and stumbling without light.

*

Inhale.
Exhale.

John Lincoln Braithwaite fondly remembers a brief visit to St Thomas Becket's Church on the Romney Marshes. This tiny, defiant structure, surrounded by a chaotic jigsaw of uneven fields; inconvenient snippets of rough pasture, each cut and divided by haywire ditches rinsed in claggy water, intersected by ramshackle bridges. Grazing sheep. Thistles. Reeds. Achingly quiet. Sudden whispering-wind-whistle. Drying molehills. The whiff of sparrowhawk.

And inside this humble yet unapologetically present brick structure? The light! Oh God, the infinite play of light! Like a celestial hymn, a transcendent hum. Shifting shafts of modest, virgin-bride marsh-light. Misty and innocent. Incomparably lovely and ethereal.

When he thinks about St Thomas Becket's Church on the Romney Marshes it's almost as if John Lincoln Braithwaite is thinking about a lover – a relationship; some special soul or entity with whom he once shared something immensely powerful and intimate. It's difficult to articulate.

LOVE

Suffice to say that his relationship to light is more than simply aesthetic. It is necessary. It is emotional. It is spiritual. It is profoundly rich and immensely deep.

Because John Lincoln Braithwaite thinks so often and so intensely about the light and the absence of light (its eternal dance, its infinite variety), his room (the room he rents in this Kentish cathedral town – just one of several rooms that he habitually rents in small towns) has been selected entirely on the basis of its relationship to the dawn and the sunset.

The dawn and the sunset are sacred. Especially the dawn, because the dawn is the start of things. The dawn is the morning's first grumbling yawn of light. He loves the dawn. He waits for it, smoking, impatient, lovelorn.

A gentle, tender yearning.

Does John Lincoln Braithwaite hate the darkness? No! Not entirely. Because without the inky-velvety-mole-fur of night there could be no end of night, surely? And no slither of moon? Or pinprick of stars? Without the absence of light there could be no light, and for this reason John Lincoln Braithwaite is a sober respecter of the darkness. He tips his cap patiently and placidly to the darkness.

Oh yes. He is real. John Lincoln Braithwaite is real. He is actually a staunch defender of the real (or a staunch defender of his perception of the real, at the very least).

The library is real. What could be more real than a library (more honest than a library? More solid and real and honest than library books?)? John Lincoln Braithwaite goes to the library and he borrows books. He owns a real library card (okay – he owns a real library card, digitally, on his phone). He owns several real library cards (okay, so he is a card-carrying member of several libraries digitally) because he prefers not to possess things but rather to honour them. He prefers to borrow books and then to carefully return them. He loves light and he lives light.

John Lincoln Braithwaite is John Lincoln Braithwaite (digitally) on his library card(s). He was always called John Lincoln Braithwaite by his mother. His mother, a single mother, held down three jobs but she still found the time to drawl out five syllables every time she called his name. That was how she honoured him, and honoured herself, as his mother. Deep inside of him is an unspeakable and unspoken love of those five syllables, and (quite naturally) a correspondingly unspeakable and unspoken loathing of them. It's complicated – his relationship to these five syllables. Too much desire and hope and expectation, too much loneliness and need and disappointment is tangled up in those five laborious syllables. But they are his and he owns them. He is brave like that. He is bolshy like that.

Fuck it, though.

That's his attitude.

Fuck it, though.

John Lincoln Braithwaite is like a leading character in a bad 1980s American capitalist drama (say *Dallas*: the indulged younger brother, the prodigal son who returns to the oil field and promises his tough yet paradoxically indulgent slate-eyed, tan-faced father that he will learn the trade from the ground up; prove himself). But he is also like a character from an excellent, slightly clunky but extremely sincere first play about a demoralised primary school teacher who is struggling to nurture a gifted but troubled Irish Traveller child written

by a 23-year-old northern prodigy whose uncle once ran (and possibly still runs) an abattoir.
Yes. Both of these things.

He reads real books. John Lincoln Braithwaite reads real books methodically and respectfully, from beginning to end (although there will sometimes be the slamming down of books accompanied by muttered expostulations or sharp exhalations – the odd well-chosen swear word – the occasional cluck or tut). He nevertheless reads books from cover to cover. He does not flip to the final page in a sudden moment of impatience. He is disciplined. He is respectful of books in the way that he is respectful of people and in the way that he is *not* respectful of live music performances.
Why is this?
It's unknown. It's a mystery.
Although there *will* be a reason, surely? Some triggering experience that taught him that it was important to leave (or politely – *always* politely – object to) a live event if something feels vaguely 'off'.

Is he aware of this little inconsistency, this small kink hidden within his consumption of culture?
Very possibly. Possibly not. Although very possibly. But this little inconsistency is not as important as smoking which is fire-watching. Not nearly as important as that. And not nearly as important as the celebration of light and the waiting for the light and the watching of the light, which is of paramount (*paramount*) importance.

*

John Lincoln Braithwaite will habitually listen to an album from start to finish (generally twice) before deciding whether or not he will invest his hard-earned cash in it. He pays real, *actual* money for things. He does not 'borrow' or steal 'content'. He is a decent man. He reads music (and literary and film) reviews in newspapers and magazines and decides what he will devote his time and his energy to. If he likes the way in which the critic has described the work – how angry or delighted it has made them feel – then he will tentatively explore the relevant cultural artefact. He despises algorithms. He does not want to be told how to consume (or what to feel) in accordance with some finite sequence of data, a series of inferences, an automated calculation. He senses that culture is a conversation – a series of clumsy nudges and mis-steps – and likes it to be a shock, a revelation. He is not interested in quiet affirmations or comforting confirmations. He must be challenged.

John Lincoln Braithwaite must *be* challenged and also feels a correspondingly deep need *to* challenge. He is an active, thinking interlocutor. He is perfectly happy to be carried (back and forth – like Mallory's metaphorical seagull, feeding in the sea-swell) on the tide of opinion, but then he will make a decision, and that decision is definitive. There is no slithering around in the comments sections of newspaper websites. None of that. Fie on that most crushing kind of power which is actually no-power and all-power! Fie on the vicious, knee-jerk, bubonic-plague-carrying rat-squeak-of-rage, the stray-cat-suddenly-neurotically-furiously-frantically-blankly-scratch-scratch-scratching! Grrr! Fur flying. Followed by obsessive licking. Followed by . . . um . . . nothing. Empty gaze. Slight whisker twitch. Fie on that! Fie!

'Excuse me.'

John Lincoln Braithwaite glances up. He is currently sitting, in a small pool of light, on a municipal bench in front of the library, smoking, thinking.

A woman and a child stand before him.

He inspects the woman and the child and says nothing. Is there really any need to respond, verbally, when a person excuses themselves?

John Lincoln Braithwaite is a signatory to the manifesto that if you can't improve on The Silence then just don't bother opening your mouth. Silence is such a lovely thing. Such a powerful thing. Who could possibly hope to improve on silence?

Although . . .

What about the lone bagpipe player at a funeral leading the coffin from church to graveside? His mother's final request (although his mother was not officially Scottish, but *Braveheart* was her favourite film). Hmm. The lone bagpipe player. Does the lone bagpipe player improve on the silence? Might he make an exception for the lone bagpipe player?

Ahhh. That's a tricky one.

Yes.

That's a tough one.

Um. Surely it's all just context . . .? The bagpipe is a grown-up instrument. Keening. Needy. If this child (for example) who stands before him were to die and be buried, would it not seem crass and excessive to play a bagpipe at her funeral (he double-checks the child's gender)? Would it not be too much? Too florid? Perhaps the bagpipe is only fitting at the . . .

'Are you TonyInterruptor?' the woman asks, slightly impatient.

TonyInterruptor frowns and takes another drag on his cigarette.

What kind of a question is that?

He exhales smoke from the side of his mouth.

TonyInterruptor?

Who . . .?

'I just want you to know that I researched it, online,' the woman continues, 'and there is nothing intrinsically fascistic or whatever about a handshake. Nothing at all. The handshake is tribal. It's a gesture of peace. It's a way of indicating to a stranger that you aren't hiding any weapons by offering them your empty palms.'

She shows him her empty palms. Her wrists are so thin it astonishes him.

TonyInterruptor gazes at Mallory Shore's palms, in silence. Who on earth is this woman?

What is she saying? More importantly, what is she interrupting?

Um.

Yes.

She is interrupting his peace. His silence.

He thinks about responding for a moment and then simply can't be bothered. No. This is too much. It's silly. Because he is just sitting outside the library, smoking and watching the light. And now someone he has never met before is standing in front of him, showing him her open palms and continuing/pursuing/trespassing upon an insignificant conversational exchange from the night before. A conversation which he found tedious (at best) and which he never even started in the first place.

How odd.

How irritating and strange.

He carefully adjusts the small pile of library books that are balanced on his lap. The top one – a hardback – has a clean white cover with a large black feather stretching from corner to corner, at a diagonal. *The Aphorisms of Franz Kafka*.

Perhaps this is all just a dream? He glances up again and inspects the play of light on the side of the woman's face and on her scalp. She has no hair.

Why no hair? Or just a centimetre of hair?

Like Sinéad O'Connor.

Sandy, brown hair. Her skin is a pleasing pale coffee colour. She is tall and thin with deep-set eyes and a strong nose. High cheekbones. She is surprisingly attractive. She has a pencil tucked behind one ear (how is that pencil managing to stay in place?) and she is wearing a huge Malian indigo-cloth scarf and a baggy, floor-length denim smock. The child has a muddy T-shirt and raggle-taggle locks, no shoes and a mesmerising stream of dried snot running from both of her nostrils.

Yes. This encounter seems too unlikely to be real. Just . . . yes . . . too unlikely. Improbable.

'And as for you,' the woman continues (now addressing a person who appears to be seated on the bench beside him), 'back to school, madam! Right now! This whole thing is weird and deeply inappropriate. It stops here.'

John Lincoln Braithwaite turns to inspect the person who is supposedly behaving weirdly and inappropriately (surely the woman herself is behaving weirdly and inappropriately?).

Okay. A teenage girl. She is small and thin and wearing an oversized black and pink hoodie (the hood pulled up) and oversized bleached jeans. White trainers with platform heels. Her face is clean of make-up but her lashes are false and enormous. Giant and spidery. He recognises her as the girl at the gig from the previous night.

'Are you actually tracking me on my phone again, Mallory?' the girl demands. 'After everything that happened last time? Are you seriously, *actually* tracking me on my phone again?'

Then, before the hairless woman has a chance to respond: 'I'm very sorry,' she continues, 'but from where I'm currently sitting *you* are the one being weird and deeply inappropriate here.'

(Bravo, John Lincoln Braithwaite thinks, bravo!)

Mallory is not impressed (John Lincoln Braithwaite suspects that little impresses Mallory. Mallory seems like a hard egg to crack. She is . . . what's the right word? Formidable?

Ha! Good luck, kid, he thinks).

'I already messaged your dad,' Mallory snaps back. 'You are fifteen years old, *India*,' (sarcastic emphasis on *India*) 'and you should be at school, LEARNING THINGS, not hanging around the town centre with some creepy stranger three times your age.'

John Lincoln Braithwaite raises his eyebrows.

Hanging around?

Creepy?

'We are *not* hanging around!' India Shore exclaims, indignant, 'I AM JUST SITTING HERE! You are *so* embarrassing. You are literally *so* fucking embarrassing. AND FOR YOUR INFORMATION THIS IS A LIBRARY! A CENTRE OF LEARNING!!'

India gesticulates dramatically towards the library with both arms outstretched, and this gesture seems to draw all of the authority, physical solidity and intellectual aspirations of this building into line with her argument.

The library is now hers. Its moral stature is now hers.

O-o-o-kay.

John Lincoln Braithwaite glances up to see Mallory's response to the 'fucking'.

'Fuck *you*, India,' Mallory counters, coolly.

Oops.

Not what he'd expected. John Lincoln Braithwaite looks back at India to gauge her reaction.

'Did you hear that?' India turns to TonyInterruptor, '*Swearing* in front of my sister?! Swearing in front of Gunn who is EIGHT YEARS OLD?! Did you *hear* that?! What kind of a mother *are* you?!' India gasps, 'Is it any wonder I'm compelled to find my own meaning if *this* is my example? IT'S DISGUSTING.'

Find my own meaning?! John Lincoln Braithwaite looks to India's sister. The child. Gunn? The child seems strangely disconnected and yet mildly entertained by everything. Mildly entertained by the entire world. Hmm. This is a laudable attitude, he thinks.

'All this tedious posturing, India,' Mallory says, 'it bores me to death.'

Ouch. John Lincoln Braithwaite winces.

'*Nobody* else says shit like that to their kids!' India gasps, 'Nobody! It's . . . I literally have NO WORDS!'

'Oh yeah, of course, *defy* the rules until someone has the nerve to call you out on it,' Mallory snorts, 'then refer *cravenly* to the rules with an unwavering sense of self-righteousness.'

John Lincoln Braithwaite frowns as he tries to work out the logic of this statement. Defy the rules until . . .?

India springs to her feet (she *has* worked out the logic and it has hit home. She is mortally wounded): 'THIS IS NOT A COURT OF LAW!' she bellows.

'YOU ARE NOT MY JUDGE AND JURY, MALLORY.'

Mallory is unmoved: 'Gunn has her speech therapy session in approximately . . .' Mallory inspects her Apple watch, 'seven minutes' time, but we can happily trail you around town for the next three hours if that's what it's going to take to get you back to school. The choice is yours.'

'I *AM* GOING BACK TO SCHOOL BECAUSE YOU MAKE MY SKIN CRAWL!'

India yells.

She glances down at John Lincoln Braithwaite.

'This is abuse,' she says, 'parading as CONCERN!'

'Parading as *care*,' Mallory corrects her. 'This is abuse parading as *care*.'

'ALWAYS THE LAST WORD!' India expostulates, storming off. 'PSYCHOTIC!'

'Surely *that* was a valiant attempt at the last word you little hypocrite!' Mallory calls after her.

(John Lincoln Braithwaite isn't entirely convinced that this is either abuse *or* care, and yes, re the last word. That seems pretty definitive. Although . . .)

'I hate this town,' Mallory announces, 'I hate the library. I hate that bench. I hate the cathedral. I even hate *you*, in this moment, and all of that . . . urgh . . . all of that . . . that pointless, effete, highbrow sanctimoniousness-ness-ness.'

Really? *Effete?!*

John Lincoln Braithewaite blinks.

Sanctimoniousness-ness-ness?

Mallory grabs the child's hand and strides off, with purpose, then pauses, just before she's fully out of earshot, and fires over her shoulder, 'Just trying to be *honest* here, Tony!'

5

Lambert Shore has cornered Fi Kinebuchi in the staffroom. He is clutching his phone.

'Did you see this, Fi?' he asks, slightly concerned, helpfully holding out the phone for her to scrutinise.

'Hello Lambert,' Fi smiles, ignoring the phone. For some reason she feels uncomfortable around Lambert Shore. She isn't entirely sure why, because Lambert is obviously a perfectly nice, polite, well-educated, charming and attractive middle-aged married man with two children. Yes. And he dresses beautifully. Conventionally and possibly a bit prissily, but . . . well. And he is still (although middle-aged) very interested in things – *engaged* . . . enga*ging*. He still carries this atmosphere of . . . this artlessness, this simple-heartedness. He seems extremely passionate. Extremely open, yet immensely cultured.

The perfect consumer. Is that right? Consumer? She

suddenly thinks of the dedication to Salinger's *Raise High the Roof Beam, Carpenters*. How does it go?

'If there is an amateur reader still left in the world – or anybody who just reads and runs . . .'

Yes. The amateur reader. The amateur listener. The amateur watcher. The person who just reads and runs. No hidden ambition, no 'doing of an opinion', just good-natured (but intelligent) appreciation. This is Lambert Shore. There's a sense of gentleness and gratitude with almost no agenda.

Oh I don't know . . . Fi Kinebuchi winces. Why is it, then, that Lambert Shore makes her feel so ridiculously . . . awkward. Jumpy. *Hot*. For this reason she always has to fight a powerful urge to rush off, immediately, on his approach. It's possible (and she loathes this thought) that she is simply *besotted* by Lambert Shore (his decency, his good looks – it's probably just something . . . urgh . . . stupid and *chemical*) and that she feels intrinsically unsafe around the inexplicably high levels of attraction he apparently holds for her.

Two things that give her pause, here: the first is that if *she* finds him irresistible then surely so does everybody else, and the idea of queuing up to . . . to validate this idiotic man's high opinion of himself (although he doesn't seem to be especially idiotic *or* over-confident) infuriates her because surely she (Fi Kinebuchi) is better and more interesting than that? Surely she is more considered and nuanced and evolved than that?

The second thing? Um. Oh! The idea that she shouldn't have to *fight* to be attracted. That she shouldn't need to investigate and assess and rootle around looking for ways to love someone *in spite of* . . . I don't know . . . in spite of what a complicated, unsteady, unpredictable creature they are. That it should all just be so . . . so *obvious*. So basic. Yes. Chemical. So base. So physical. Nothing intellectual, nothing fought for, nothing special, just something immediately felt and deeply *understood*. No . . . Grrr. It's too much! Embarrassing. Uncontrolled. And it's ridiculous. Ridiculous! And unexpected. It takes her by surprise. It makes her burn with . . . with a kind of unfamiliar *stiffness* and clumsiness and . . .

It's unsafe. So she wants to run (heavily – like a big clown in big clown boots – possibly tripping up). And maybe write a song. Or a poem. Then groan (like some giant underwater mammalian) and throw a cushion against a wall.

Lambert Shore is deeply impressed by Fi Kinebuchi. To Lambert Shore, Fi Kinebuchi is a true artist. She is the real deal. She is authentically bohemian without even knowing it. Not in a 'wearing of bright colours and designer glasses' way. Not in an 'attending Life Drawing classes and baking sourdough bread' way. But sincerely. Her blouses! Synthetic. Giant collars. Beige. Or brown. *Brown!* Buttons sometimes missing! The occasional safety pin. Her strange skirts which do everything possible not to flatter her (apparently, possibly, maybe) curvaceous figure. A love of brooches (brooches!) and expanses of leather twine suspending large, strange pottery pendants. There is one: oval, green, featuring two clumsily etched naked figures – pre-pubescent male and female – holding hands. The way it bounces off her breasts as she walks!

Her choices seem so odd and skewed to Lambert Shore (whose own choices strike him – and quite rightly – as anything *but* odd and skewed) that they imply a person utterly indifferent to the male gaze (to *any* gaze). A quietness and a confidence. A self-contained-ness.

She is a pure soul. To Lambert Shore, Fi Kinebuchi is the very model of integrity. An exotic flower – an orchid – in the mundane greenhouse of the staffroom (that greenhouse full of mini-cucumbers and radishes – Lambert himself is a Moneymaker tomato; ripened to an unnaturally bright hue on a constant drip-diet of Baby Bio).

'Oh. Um. Yes. Sorry. Hello Fi.'

He winces.

Too formal one minute (with TonyInterruptor) then not sufficiently formal the next?!

Lambert pauses. *Was* he being too familiar? Too entitled? Approaching Fi Kinebuchi like that? Presumably Fi Kinebuchi gets slightly irritated by people (like him), fans (like him), just approaching her (this rare orchid) willy-nilly, holding out their phones like idiots. Like clumsy, entitled, devouring idiots.

His tongue suddenly feels huge in his mouth.

That's weird.

Fi Kinebuchi is now wrangling her giant mane of hair between her two graceful but distinctly un-manicured hands. She is fixing her hair, with an immense amount of skill and a deeply businesslike air. The hair needs to be tied back RIGHT NOW, it seems. This is an ABSOLUTE IMPERATIVE.

Fi Kinebuchi is a big presence (although not an overwhelming or demanding presence), but she is very tiny. Lambert Shore is a short man. Not tiny, but not tall. When he stands next to Fi Kinebuchi he feels like a brute. She is like a field mouse. Fi Kinebuchi is like a field mouse who scampers up a single stalk of ripened yellow wheat with inordinate levels of speed and dexterity, then waits at the top, assaying the world with its intense but innocent rodent eyes. Tiny as anything. Light as anything. Natural as anything.

Lambert Shore looks on in astonishment, marvelling at the beautiful way in which Fi Kinebuchi wrangles her wild mane of hair with so much effortlessness and finesse. He has often wondered at her ethnicity. What are the actual (and the literal) roots of that amazing mane? Kinebuchi! Such an interesting name!

(For the record, Fi's maiden name was originally Butler. Kinebuchi was deftly hijacked from her first husband – a marriage that lasted only three months in total – when she was seventeen.)

Lambert quietly observes as Fi just ... woah ... kind of *throws* her hair between her two hands (like a pizza chef deftly manhandling soft balls of dough) and then twizzles it around and ties it in a knot. *There are no rubber bands or pins to hold it in place! Nature holds it in place!* The hair simply stays where she puts it! It seems to have its own ... what would the word be? Its own ... I don't know. What would that word be?

Lambert Shore is a professor of architecture! Structures, construction, building materials etc. are his business! This is ridiculous!

Wiriness?

He can't, for the life of him, think of the word. Fi Kinebuchi has frozen his brain with her fragrant proximity!

Oh.

What *is* her fragrance, exactly?

Violin resin. Espresso coffee. Mothballs. Musk.

Gosh.

His frozen brain fizzles, overstimulated.

Tensile?

Is that it? There is definitely a word for exactly this scenario. A word that perfectly describes Fi Kinebuchi's strangely . . . uh . . . something (the word) hair.

Fi Kinebuchi has tied up her hair (and is patently trying to disguise her unease at the proximity of Lambert Shore by busying herself with this little task) but now realises that her hair is no longer operating as a screen behind which she can hide her face – especially her cheeks, which feel hot – from Lambert Shore's close scrutiny.

This is a dreadful realisation for Fi Kinebuchi. Fi Kinebuchi is a performer for heaven's sake! But she is actually very shy. Underneath it all. The performance is the shield of confidence that she brandishes ahead of her. She can easily hide behind her autoharp, her lute, her guitar; the technique, the formality, the sound.

Fi Kinebuchi stares at Lambert Shore for a second, panicked, unblinking, and then promptly puts up her hands and takes down her hair from its band-and-pinless bun.

She feels like a complete idiot.

Lambert Shore is privileged to watch Fi Kinebuchi's amazing dexterity again, and to see how that magnificently assembled bun can be deconstructed just as quickly and simply as it was formerly constructed. It just . . . Wooo! It just *comes apart*! It falls. It collapses into wild curls again, just as wonderfully. It's actually . . . as an architect . . . a person interested in construction and in art . . . it's actually . . . I don't know . . . humbling . . . to see something go up and then come down so exquisitely, so naturally. It brings tears to his eyes. It actually brings tears to his eyes! Literal tears!

Lambert Shore blinks. Fi Kinebuchi stares at him, unblinking, through her mane of hair. Lambert Shore admires Fi Kinebuchi so much in this moment that he feels like baring his soul to her because Fi Kinebuchi can understand souls and the bearing of souls since this is her business, as an artist. This is her everyday language. And this is why she is beautiful and unique. She trades in souls.

This is also a perfect opportunity for Lambert Shore to be a bit of an artist himself (Lambert Shore is no artist. Absolutely not. He just . . . he just isn't. He lacks the essential . . . the basic *stuff*) by being absolutely soulful and transparent with Fi Kinebuchi. This is his privilege, right now, in the staffroom: a precious chance to just . . . just *turn up* (emotionally) and say precisely what he feels.

'It literally brought a tear to my eye,' he murmurs, 'to see you tie up and take down your hair. Just . . . without . . .' He gestures, helplessly.

'Sorry?' Fi Kinebuchi is certain that she can't possibly have heard him correctly. What the hell is he talking about? And why exactly does he want her to look at his phone?

'Without pins. Your hair,' he says, 'um . . . tensile. Sorry . . . not the right . . . The way you just . . . just throw it up like that, and you don't need any . . . any pins.'

'Tensile?'

Fi Kinebuchi is astonished by this. Her automatic need (her overwhelming urge) is to rapidly tie up her hair again because she requires something to do with her hands, but that would obviously be completely ridiculous – almost insane – at this juncture.

'Tensile,' he continues, faltering, 'it's almost . . . you know, tensile. Perhaps that's the wrong word?'

'Tensile,' Fi Kinebuchi echoes again, as if mesmerised by the word, then, 'Tensile?' she repeats, with a question mark.

Lambert Shore is suddenly full of regret. He's embarrassed. Fi Kinebuchi sees this and feels bad because she is naturally very kind.

'I was just thinking about the dedication to *Raise High the Roof Beam, Carpenters*,' she burbles. 'It's about the amateur reader: "If there is an amateur reader still left in the world – or anybody who just reads and runs . . ."

'I don't know why it popped into my head. I've always really liked and admired it – the title – but I can never quite remember the context . . . what it . . . what it *means.* It just feels like a random collection of words . . . or simply an idea . . . the *idea* of a title which perfectly fulfils its intellectual and emotional brief through mere rhythm and sound . . . *Raise High the Roof Beam, Carpenters . . .*' she incants, 'Or not even that. It's evasive – purposefully obscure. It refuses to be instantly decoded. I don't know. It feels cryptic and enigmatic and abstruse . . .' She suddenly stops burbling. (Hang on! Is she actually just describing *herself* here? Cryptic? Enigmatic? Um . . .)

Lambert Shore is gazing at her, utterly entranced. Can that be right? She glances over her shoulder. Is there someone . . .? Might there be somebody standing directly . . .?

No. Nobody behind her. Fi Kinebuchi clears her throat, nervously, 'But then I instantly start to wonder if it's just me . . . if it's just me who doesn't bother to try and pick apart the meaning of it – Salinger's literal, actual intention – but prefers to learn it, almost by rote, because I lack the focus or . . . or . . . or *intelligence* – which surely amounts to the same thing . . .?'

'What an incredible woman,' Lambert Shore murmurs. What he actually means to say is 'what an incredible *man* [i.e. J. D. Salinger]', but his tongue slips. Because he finds Fi Kinebuchi incredible, and she is standing right here, in front of him, with all of her virtuosity and her strangeness and her hair.

'Sorry?' Fi Kinebuchi starts (understandably).

'I meant "man" . . . apologies . . . I meant "what an

incredible *man*". He was. Salinger. What an incredible *man*. It's probably slightly idiotic, but I always naturally . . . automatically . . . instinctively think of him as the shadow-side of Warhol – who represents pure post-modern cynicism – in his persistent, dogged pursuit of . . . of . . . well, *heart*.'

'Yes! The amateur reader. The amateur listener,' Fi Kinebuchi nods, repeating herself as she makes this connection. 'The amateur watcher. The person who just reads and runs . . .' She pauses, frowning.

'What an incredibly [she is now unconsciously mirroring Lambert Shore in her use of language, because she is attracted to him] interesting point you make there,' she muses. 'Was the Salinger dedication much earlier?'

'I imagine so,' Lambert Shore nods. 'I believe the book was published in the mid-fifties. Warhol's infamous "15 minutes" was first used in an exhibition brochure in the late sixties – 1967 or 1968 . . .'

'So ten years earlier and Salinger was already reading the cultural climate and deciding . . . feeling this deep resistance, this sense of foreboding, in his gut . . .'

'I would hate to trespass into the sphere of mansplaining,' Lambert continues, nervously, 'but if I remember correctly, the title – the *Roof Beam Carpenters* title – is actually a line . . . a fragment . . . from a song. It comes from an old hymn which one of the characters uses as part of a wedding speech to congratulate the book's hero . . . I don't know . . . I could be wrong . . . but I think it's something like that. So as a title it's *meant* to feel sort of quotable and yet meaningless at the same time, I suspect. Your instincts are ... your intuition is probably ... typically ... spot on.'

'A whole decade!'

Fi is astonished. 'And Salinger is already feeling as if nobody can just ... just ...'

She struggles to find the word.

'... innocently consume ...' Lambert says.

'No ... no ... consume is exactly the *wrong* word ...' Fi corrects him, frowning.

'Of course.'

'I mean it's *consumption* that makes Salinger write the dedication ... this desire he has to use art simply to ... um ... to engage in a way that is sincere and spontaneous and wholesome ... not something considered and cynical and ... and *vampiric* ...'

She winces at the very thought.

'You're right ...' Lambert nods, understanding, 'Capitalism depends on – subsists by – turning art into commerce, monetising it rather than allowing it to be something pure and beautiful that enriches the soul ...'

'*Oh bugger!*' Fi suddenly interrupts him, at a whisper, her jaw stiffening. '*Jane Finch approaching!*'

'Sorry?'

Lambert gazes at Fi, blankly, then glances over his shoulder. Jane Finch is head of English. Lambert and Mallory Shore are both good pals with Jane Finch.

'Are we talking about Salinger?' Jane Finch demands, gate-crashing their tête-à-tête, apparently without compunction (Jane Finch wrote a dissertation at Oxford about Salinger which was later turned into a very poor student film).

'Um . . . yes . . . just . . . just the title: *Raise High the Roof Beam, Carpenters* . . .' Lambert explains, 'I was telling Fi that it originally came from a song . . . a hymn . . .'

Lambert Shore notices Fi Kinebuchi visibly shrink at Jane Finch's proximity. Really?! Does . . . does Fi Kinebuchi fear or . . . or *dislike* Jane Finch? But who could possibly fear or dislike . . .?

Oh.

'Good heavens, no,' Jane Finch frowns, 'That's completely wrong, Lambert. It's actually a quote from Sappho . . .'

Fi Kinebuchi, like clockwork, promptly commences re-arranging her hair.

Lambert turns back to Fi, blinks twice, then suddenly finds himself clumsily improvising (as if determined to protect their little Salinger exchange from all of Jane Finch's vile accuracy and certainty and clarity *at any cost*), 'To um . . . film you *putting up your hair* . . .' he stutters, 'because it's a natural form of . . . of architecture. A kind of . . . an . . . um . . . an . . . a sort of intuitive construction.'

'Hair?' Jane Finch echoes, confused.

'A . . . um . . . film. A *series* of films of . . . women . . . people . . . people of all genders . . .' Lambert stumbles.

'You want to film Fi *putting up her hair?*'

Jane Finch is intrigued.

'Yes. Without pins. An intuitive construction. But not

just . . . not just Fi. A series of films. I was asking Fi if she knew of any other women who . . . *people* who . . .'

'There *is* a salon,' Fi nods, instantly catching on (improvisation is her forte, after all), 'in London. They only cut curly hair. It's a dedicated salon. It's very expensive and I rarely have the time or the resources to . . .'

'That sounds great. I mean it's obviously just a very . . . a very . . . um . . .'

Fi nods, '. . . embryonic . . .'

'Yes, *embryonic . . . preliminary . . .*'

'Good heavens. I had no idea you were thinking of moving into the arena of *video art*, Lambert,' Jane scoffs, highly entertained.

'Well, yes. Yes. It was just . . . I don't know . . . just a thought. Nothing. Nothing set in stone.'

'Wow.' Jane looks equivalently bemused and amused.

Perhaps Jane Finch *is* a tiny bit supercilious, Lambert thinks. I mean is it *that* improbable for someone like him – someone pedestrian and middle-aged and boring like him – to aspire to . . . to . . .?

'Did you see all the stuff on Instagram this morning, Fi?' Jane Finch promptly (and brutally) changes tack. She holds out her phone.

'Pardon?'

Fi is disconcerted.

Lambert glowers at Jane Finch, even though she has just asked *exactly* the question he himself was planning to ask (or had asked) Fi Kinebuchi on his first approach. Before all the . . . the Salinger and the hair stuff which has obviously . . . I don't know . . . transformed their interaction into something . . . something loftier . . . something . . .

'Might I possibly just have a very quick word with you, Jane?' Lambert suddenly finds himself abruptly turning and blocking the objectionable Jane Finch (and her phone) from Fi. His abruptness is countered by him gently (very gently) taking her by the arm and swiftly escorting her to the coffee machine; 'It's about our timetable clash on Wednesday morning . . .'

Timetable clash?

Are Lambert Shore and Jane Finch not professors in *entirely different* departments?

Fi Kinebuchi doesn't need telling twice. She turns on her adorable rodent heel and scampers from the staffroom.

Yes, for the record she *does* know about all the fuss on Instagram. And X. And . . . and . . . She *does* know. But she honestly can't tell how she feels about it, currently (there has been no reposting on her pages at this point, and no particular urge to repost, either).

Fi Kinebuchi rarely enters the staffroom (this most stuffy, oppressive and competitive of spaces), so why enter the staffroom today of all days? Why would she . . .? I don't know. Perhaps in order to surreptitiously gauge if anything *in the real world* (the solid world, the true world, OUT THERE) has visibly shifted? So that she is able, at some level, to confirm to herself that this crazy online stuff is actually . . . well, *serious*? Because it all seems so . . . so strange and blinkered and unnecessary. And she keeps seeing all these versions of herself, popping up, without prompting, on her tiny screen, and she honestly doesn't understand what it signifies. Surely they can't *all* (all these versions, these opinions) be pertinent or necessary?

And the sheer numbers? These improbably high numbers of likes and reposts? And the comments? The righteous indignation? The avalanche of support, of sympathy? Then, finally, the slew (the inevitable slew) of criticism? Of hate?

Do they translate into something actual? Or is the world's attention span simply too short (and are the mechanisms of technology simply too fast) for it to imply anything palpable or significant? Anything true?

Yes. In summary. That sounds about . . . about right. That seems about . . . about right.

Fi Kinebuchi scampers towards the music department. Will Lemmy (the music tech guy) have seen . . .? Might he . . .? Oh dear.

She unknots her hair from its loose bun. Her cheeks are glowing. Is she being completely paranoid or are some of the students sniggering and surreptitiously pointing her way?

(She *is* being completely paranoid. And some of the students *are* surreptitiously sniggering and pointing her way.) Hang on.

Fi Kinebuchi grinds to a sudden halt.

Did Lambert Shore just step in to save her from the

occupational hazard/train-crash that is/was Jane Finch back there?
Is Lambert Shore her friend, now? Her ally?
Are they pals?
Lambert Shore and Fi Kinebuchi?

'INTUITIVE CONSTRUCTION'
?!?!

Because isn't that how friends behave?
They help each other out in times of need? They confide in each other? They save each other (shield each other) from their mortal enemies?

Her heart lurches. Then she surely and swiftly reprimands her heart.
Grrr. Stop it! Grrr! *Grrrr!* Naughty heart! Wayward heart! *Foolish* heart!

6

‘It’s just a question of how the hell we get the damn puppet *back* into the box again at this stage, Sasha. Because once the puppet is out of its box . . .’

Sasha Keyes is Zooming with his redoubtable, self-styled ‘lady-manager’, Janice ‘Lacey’ Hinde. Lacey is a 61-year-old former Goth (she once had a stall at Hyper Hyper and made T-shirts for Marc Almond) who still sometimes crimps her hair, always wears her trademark lace, and invariably (because she is constructed like a small but perfectly upholstered battleship) leads with her bust.

‘Sorry, Lacey,’ Sasha interrupts, ‘but on a purely . . . I mean, just for the sake of clarity, a puppet – or a ‘jack’ – is physically *designed* to go back into its box. If what you’re attempting to say here is that the genie is out of the *lamp* . . .’

Lacey Hinde is possibly the only person on the planet to whom Sasha Keyes will – on the odd, rare occasion – defer.

She is formidable (both personally and in business), being at once magnificently dynamic, utterly mercenary and unequivocally brutal.

'I'm not.' (Lacey is typically uncompromising.) 'If the genie were out of the lamp then we could simply "wish" your problems away . . .' (confidently timed pause) '. . . and I fear we cannot simply wish your problems away, my friend.'

'Perhaps if we just ditch the puppet idea altogether and focus on the box? A *Pandora's* box . . .?'

Sasha is plainly impressed – almost shaken – by the pause. As a musician he fully understands how much bravery is invested in a successful pause.

'This is a perfect example of what gets you into trouble, Sash,' Lacey rolls her eyes (while carefully adjusting her black boned bodice with an exquisitely manicured red talon).

'What? *What?!* My specificity?' Sasha rocks back on his chair in astonishment and his head is temporarily lost in a balaclava of fuzz. 'You're saying my specificity – my pursuit of excellence – is the problem here . . .?!'

(the head reconsolidates)

'Why? Simply because I happen to be *invested* in details – in facts – in a world where nobody gives a damn any more about expertise or precision or accuracy . . .?'

'Yes, yes,' Lacey nods emphatically. 'Your terrible perfectionism and legendary irascibility are part and parcel of what make you a brilliantly charismatic and uncompromising musician and performer, but they are also your Achilles heel: your key area of vulnerability. It is – quite frankly – a source

of constant wonder and astonishment to me that you've somehow managed to evade a public flogging hence-far.'
(Lacey is satisfied that she has now clearly demonstrated a working understanding of Greek mythology in spite of – or perhaps because of – Sasha's former belittling. By coincidence, she has a 15-year-old son called Myrrh who is really into Greek myths. It's a thing among teens. Why might this be? She often speculates on the subject. She suspects it's because of the wider culture's increasing indifference to the once useful moral and metaphorical scaffolding of the Judeo-Christian tradition. She shudders to think how Punks or Goths would've managed in the cultural wastelands of the seventies and eighties without those trusty, dusty old Christians to define themselves against.

Yet now, because tried-and-tested moral tropes like 'Do as you would be done unto . . . ' and drab but reliable parables like The Good Samaritan have fallen into disuse – or, worse still, have been hijacked by the lunatic Christian Right – kids are compelled to grub around and find their spiritual consolation at Hogwarts, with the Vikings, or among the deliciously gender-fluid Greeks . . .)

'To dare call me out for not being *honest*, when I am virtually the only person left on the planet who actually speaks their mind – *and* expresses themselves creatively – without visible constraint?!' Sasha huffs, 'Then, mere hours later,' he continues, 'to be held in an online necklock by a load of opinionated, wet-behind-the-ears millennials because I'm *too* honest after the show while being filmed, without my consent, by that opportunist dickhead Simo Treen?! I mean what the fucking fuck?!'

(Again, the sudden rocking backwards and the accompanying fuzz balaclava.)

'I can certainly detect an element of . . . of irony . . . in that summary,' Lacey concedes (Sasha notes how Lacey has used the word 'summary' rather than 'situation' in response to his cogent analysis, which kind of, well, almost stings).

'This asphyxiating culture of carefulness!' he exclaims (his irritation now expanding into a burgeoning mushroom cloud of rage), 'It pretends to be all cuddly – marching under the banner of "inclusion" and a deep concern for other people's "well-being" – but if you dare to tilt that friendly mask by so much as *an inch*, you're staring straight into the face of a New Fundamentalism, an obsession with self and the protection of self *at all or any cost*,' (he slaps his desktop, three times, for emphasis.) 'Fixed Group Identities are the new fascism, Lacey. They represent a serious threat to the whole intellectual construct of classical liberalism.'

Lacey watches Sasha kindly as he rants. She feels now – and has always felt – that Sasha is an extremely unpredictable and intermittently vicious clinically obese 17-year-old Rottweiler with mesmerisingly yellow teeth and advanced arthritis living inside the body of an inordinately pale and skinny 45-year-old suit model with a powerful jaw, giant hands and Superman-style spectacles (whose only real purpose, surely, are to be hurled off during a life-and-death crisis). She starts to construct a sentence in response, but before she can quite muster it . . .

'I mean this ludicrous attachment to "otherness",' Sasha's giant hands fly up into ironically simpering air quotes, 'which is, in actual fact, an "othering" of every poor sod who isn't a sworn-in member of your tiny clique. This sudden need – this ridiculous compulsion – to draw a sharp line around yourself, like you're some vulnerable toddler peering over the edge of its playpen! "This is who *I* am!" "This is who *you* aren't!" *Bah!* Are your psychological boundaries really so permeable?'

Lacey almost smiles at the sheer depth of Sasha's indignation (Sasha is always indignant. He was born in a state of profound indignation. His mother's breast was – she presumes – never sufficiently full of milk).

'I'm serious!' Sasha's barks, 'What *are* we all now, *AMOEBAS*?!'

(To a performer at Sasha's level of accomplishment, Lacey's almost-smile is intoxicating catnip.)

'It's inward-looking, Lacey,' he hectors, 'it's sectarian, it's clannish, it's excluding . . . And why, though? *Why?*'

(this is a rhetorical question)

'. . . because they lack the basic, human, *animal* resilience – the pluck and imagination – to stay stable – whole – within their own ridiculously fragile sense of self, which means they feel duty-bound to guard and police everything – *everything*: language, art, freedom. Their identity – their preciousness, their "other"ness, their demented particularity – becomes their sense of victimhood, their victimhood spawns self-righteousness, their self-righteousness spawns their own mealy-mouthed form of bullying. This isn't *care*, Lacey, it's solipsism . . . it's . . . it's Narcissus gazing into the pond at his own reflection and conducting a facile conversation with his own perfectly inane echo!'

Lacey attempts to speak (Ah, here we go – straight back to the sodding Greeks again . . .) but Sasha crashes on, regardless (jumping and stuttering across her screen like Marcel Delgado's stop-frame-animation King Kong going three rounds with the Empire State Building): 'It's all SO FUCKING SMALL,' he groans, 'that's what kills me! That's what torments me! It's all so cramped and careful and tethered and unimaginative! How can a person – a man – hope to be creative in this asphyxiating environment? How?! It's like they choose to live in a pond because they're threatened by THE SEA. But the sea *is* THE FUCKING SEA even if they can't tolerate the size and the scope of it, the ridiculous, jumped-up, pronoun-obsessed little nazis!'

During this extended diatribe Lacey can be intermittently heard to mutter 'Sasha? *Sash?* Sasha! *Sash!*' until finally: '*I CAN'T POSSIBLY GET DIVERTED INTO A DISCUSSION ABOUT THE POLITICS OF GENDER RIGHT NOW!*' she yells (then is visibly jolted by the unexpected volume of her own interjection). 'I'm sorry . . .' she clears her throat, 'but we have way bigger fish to fry, here . . .'

'Seriously? I hook you a whale,' Sasha's lip curls, 'and you tell me it won't fit into your frying pan?!' He throws up his hands, despairing. 'There we have it: the core of the fucking problem in a nutshell!'

'I can't – and I won't – fault your argument on metaphysical, logical or theoretical grounds, Sasha,' Lacey concedes (slightly on the back foot after her earlier loss of cool), 'unfortunately I am *a manager* and therefore a pragmatist. As an artist you have the privilege of idealism. As your manager, alas, I do not.'

Sasha gazes up at his light fitting, grimacing (but also at once reassuringly spent and sated). Ah yes, pragmatism; a wonderful concept, *on paper* (there it sits, all smug and cheerful, with its trusty stablemates Compromise and Flexibility). Yup. Helpful concepts *on paper* until you're suddenly compelled to apply them to yourself . . .

Hic!

Oops. He clears his throat. Then he hiccups again. He frowns. 'Kippers,' he announces, 'For lunch.'

He burps gently, behind his knuckles.

'If it helps at all,' Lacey admits, 'I've always felt – at a profound level – that compartmentalising . . . fixed group identities, whatever you want to call it . . . is simply a defence against paradox. And life *is* paradox, Sasha. Life is – and has always been – paradox.'

'Did you work out the legalities yet?' Sasha wonders (ignoring her point about 'paradox' because this is a relatively new concept for him which he needs time to digest . . . um . . . and he is already being plagued by acid reflux).

'Pardon?' Lacey tips her head.

Sasha leans closer into his screen and knits his giant hands together. 'The legalities. Around the issue of copyright?'

'Uh.' Lacey frowns (and finds herself instinctively pulling

back). 'What are we referring to, here? The TonyInterrupting post or the illicit backstage footage?'

'TonyInterrup*ting*,' Sasha eye-rolls (Seriously?!).

'We already tried to strong-arm India Shore – the schoolgirl,' Lacey grimaces, 'but – as luck would have it – her mother, Mallory, is a lawyer and an unholy bitch.'

'Really?' Sasha is taken aback. 'Who told you this?'

'I spoke to Fi. She works with her husband at the university.'

'Oh.'

Sasha scowls. Lacey duly notes his sullen look.

'Believe it or not,' she counsels, 'given the toe-curling nature of the online footage, Fi is actually our ally here.'

'Well, for the record, it's not Tony*Interrupting*,' Sasha clarifies (refusing, point-blank, to give Fi her due), 'it's TonyInterrup*tor*.'

'Keep your hair on,' Lacey scoffs, 'it's only a hashtag.'

'It's *my* hashtag!' Sasha is indignant, '*I* created the fucking hashtag, and – for your information – the hashtag is the only reason this whole thing has taken off.'

'You're like the blacksmith who is being kicked to death by a pony,' Lacey nods, 'and proudly points to its newly shodden hoof as he draws his final breath.'

Sasha is secretly impressed by Lacey's analogy (this is precisely why she deserves her 20%).

'The guy was just another stupid heckler until I gave him a name,' he grumbles, 'Krishnamurti says that when you teach a child that a bird is named "bird" . . .'

'Yes, yes, I watched the footage,' Lacey sighs, 'We've *all* watched the footage – approximately four hundred thousand sodding times. I can't turn on X or Instagram without seeing either some magnificently be-hashtagged heckler accusing you of being dishonest, or you telling your only female band-mate to "shut the fuck up" backstage. So yes, I think I *get* the whole Krishna-thingy idea at this point. I think we *all* get the Krishna-thingy idea at this point.'

'What tortures me is that I *created* this little prick. I've been . . .'

Words temporarily fail him.

'Hoist by your own petard?' Lacey suggests.

'. . . I've been the unwitting architect of my own demise. It's as if I plucked a handful of red clay from the river's edge, casually fashioned it into the semblance of a man and then calmly breathed life into it. He was just some idiot heckler until I created him by *naming* him.'

'Let nobody ever accuse you,' Lacey chuckles (equal parts entertained and horrified), 'of bringing anything less than 100% Main Character Energy into these situations, Sash.'

'Main character . . .?!' Sasha echoes (his sense of humour is a somewhat less developed sense than his other five).

'Did you really just pluck it from the ether, though?' Lacey sidesteps, ruthlessly, 'Wasn't it the title of an old Fall song originally?'

'How many times?!' Sasha splutters. 'That hashtag, that idea, is *mine*. I *am* the main character in this tragedy and I make no fucking apology for it. I'm the tragic fucking hero in a world – a landscape – composed *entirely* out of lies. If you are determined to talk PARADOX, Lacey, then how about trying *that* one on for size? I'm *so* honest that I can only be destroyed by the accusation of *dis*-honesty. It's an authentically Shakespearian set-up in a world where nobody reads sodding Shakespeare any more. Not only is this hashtag *my intellectual property*, it's also *my tragic flaw*.'

(Sasha studied classics at Durham University. He still staunchly insists that it's the most useful degree for negotiating the pitfalls of modern living.)

'Okay. Okay.' Lacey folds both hands, neatly, on her lap and closes her eyes in an attempt to ground herself. 'This is performers,' she thinks. 'Right here. This is why performers need managers. Because they are demented narcissists with zero common sense.' She opens her eyes again.

'I'm going to be completely candid with you, Sasha: TonyInterruptor interrupting is the very *least* of your problems right now. Simo Treen shamelessly bandwagon-jumping is what's truly sent this thing into the stratosphere. It's a perfect storm.'

'Simo Treen is – and has always been – a covetous, talentless tiny-dick,' Sasha hisses, 'I could quite happily cut his balls off.'

'As Simo's manager I am compelled to ask you not to escalate this situation,' Lacey warns.

Sasha rolls his eyes and silently curses his inordinately long-held allegiance to the punk DIY ethic. It took him fifteen unprofitable years to discover that he was signally incapable of managing himself. Lacey was Simo's manager long before she was his.

'For the sake of accuracy,' Lacey adds (and she is all about the accuracy), 'have you ever actually *seen* Simo's dick?'

'What the hell?!' Sasha is indignant.

'It's huge,' Lacey promptly answers the question for him. 'It makes no real sense, proportionately. It's extremely confusing, aesthetically.'

Sasha rests his head in his hands for a moment. 'Unbelievable. Fucking unbelievable,' he murmurs, 'I share a manager with my chief persecutor and the mother of Sally Baxter Girl Reporter is a sodding *lawyer*. Has Mel Brooks been hired to tweak this script?'

'Perhaps if we just consider the practicalities . . .' Lacey suggests.

'It's too late,' Sasha interrupts. 'I cannot hold back the giant tide of digital shit which threatens to engulf me. The tsunami of analysis, derision and hatred, of which I am the sole beneficiary, is already out there. I'm helpless in the face of it. I am fucked.'

He burps, gently, as an afterthought.

'Agreed.' Lacey doesn't sugar-coat it. 'Our only power in this situation is how we choose to respond. Do we swallow the frog, agree to do media and apologise, unreservedly – try to make amends? Do we pretend to be completely unphased by it all, stay silent and appear to take the higher ground? Do we Trump-it-out and simply deny *actual physical evidence* like complete lunatics, or pretend that the whole thing is some kind of cynical and calculated set-up – a giant practical joke – purposefully designed to draw attention to your upcoming tour?'

'That last option,' Sasha looks shocked but impressed, 'is borderline genius, but we both know that I'm an irascible old wanker with no social skills to speak of. Better if I say and do nothing,' he shrugs. 'Bollocks to it all. It's happening because of me and in spite of me.'

He falls silent for a second, then almost creaks: 'Thanks for the "we".'

Lacey is taken aback. Things must be bad. To hear Sasha . . . well, actually express *gratitude*?

'No problem, Sash,' she shrugs. 'You're sensitive. You're snappy and cantankerous. You've never suffered fools gladly, but that's a fundamental part of what permits you to be boundlessly driven and creative. We are all here because of it; me, Simo, Fi. This shitstorm is simply the inconvenient shadow-side of what makes you great.'

Sasha nods.

'And *that's* fucking honest,' she adds.

Sasha nods again. He is quiet for a moment. 'You know, Lace,' he sighs, his voice softer, now, 'the real irony is that *I* am fucking "Other". That's what haunts and torments me in moments like this. I've dedicated my whole life to outlier music. It's my world – my meaning. Improvised music has always existed on the periphery, and so have I. I'm perfectly happy to inhabit the cultural corners. I'm not interested in the smooth edges, and never have been. Experimental music

has its detractors. It's a soft target. It's difficult to like – to love. It challenges. It maddens and it confounds. We are not understood or welcomed by the cultural mainstream. They snort at – and deride – us. They belittle our obscure modes of expression. But we believe, nonetheless. We persist. We are passionate. We are scratchy. We are happily obscure. We aren't digestible ...' Sasha clutches his stomach, grimacing, 'We don't pander or pacify or anaesthetise. We are, by and large, a collection of freaks, obsessives and weirdos. And, in spite of that – or maybe even because of it – we have our own unobtrusive dignity, our own ways of engaging. We are particular. We are determined. We are persistent. We don't turn away from the difficult stuff. We won't settle. I mean do you think it's *easy* being me in an endlessly shallow, unthinking, instantly gratified and gratifying world? Expressing all the messy stuff – the jarring notes, the bad notes, the complicated flavours, the discord? Demanding concentration when nobody concentrates on anything nowadays for more than five short seconds? No. It *isn't* fucking easy. It's terrible. But my philosophy? What I say to myself every morning as I stare at my reflection in the bathroom mirror? I say, "Sasha, *if you aren't living on the edge then you are taking up too much fucking space.*"'
He shrugs, 'Gotta walk the walk if you talk the talk.'
His voice shakes a little.

'Did you come up with that yourself?' Lacey looks impressed. 'The bathroom mirror mantra?'

'Nope ...' Sasha frowns. 'I read it in an article in the *National Geographic* about an American mountaineer.'

'Ah.'

A brief and slightly awkward silence follows.

'We should just reframe this situation as an opportunity to expand and evolve artistically,' Lacey volunteers. 'We should pivot.'

Sasha inhales, deeply. 'What really messes with my head is my absolute certainty that all of the options you just offered me are *completely* wrong and – at the same time – *absolutely* right: I mean at this particular moment in history. It has never mattered more what you say – how you react – and at the same time it has never mattered less. The world is fucked, and I see no better or more sincere way of expressing this than through improvisation. There is no more fitting medium. I feel this in my *very being*. Now, more than ever, I long to grab my trumpet, slam it to my lips and *just blow.* There is a kind of . . . a kind of violent urge in me to spew out disharmony as a way of making sense and meaning out of what is irrational, contradictory, absurd, anomalous, irresistible. And that . . . that, my dear Lacey, is honourable. It's fucking *honourable.* So bollocks to the rest of it. The baaing, the bleating, the digital fucking cacophony . . .' Sasha repeatedly slams his hand down onto his thigh to hammer out his point, in syllables; 'It will pass. It. Will. Pass.'

Lacey says nothing. She just nods, which is the only response Sasha requires. Then – after a sensible lacuna – she says, 'It may interest you to know that Simo has been approached by a rather famous digital artist who intends to create some NFTs and manufacture a small number of limited-edition

T-shirts around the disputed hashtag. Considerable sums of money are involved. Might there be any taped footage in existence – not taken or created by Simo himself – of you using the term first?'

Sasha looks down for a moment. Lacey watches his face on screen, nervously. A long pause follows, then he looks up again, scowling. He adjusts the heavy glasses on his nose:

'"Swallow the frog", Lacey?' he murmurs, bemused … '*Seriously*, though?'

7

'We would've called it a "heckle".'

'A what?' India Shore scowls over at her father. She has been waiting impatiently (sitting, cross-legged, on their expensively voluminous, butter-soft tan leather living-room sofa) for the obligatory 'you shouldn't have bunked off school' lecture. Her hood is pulled up. He can only see a single, glowering eye.

'Heckle,' he repeats.

Lambert Shore suspects – actually, he knows – that India often pretends not to recognise particular words he uses simply to make it seem as if he is incredibly old and therefore given to communicating in a way that holds no significance to the modern (young) mind. He is an historical artefact, a period piece. He – and his words – are antique.

'Like cackle, but with an "h",' he explains, 'and an "e",' he adds, as an afterthought.

'Well I'm not especially bothered about how people chose

to label stuff in the olden days,' India shrugs, 'I only care about finding interesting ways of describing things *now*, ideas that are new. New ideas.'

'Just because you invent an original word for something,' Lambert reasons, 'or find an innovative way of describing it, that doesn't actually change what it truly *is* – its essential nature or purpose – especially if the old word serves perfectly well . . .'

'Dad,' India sighs, 'this was not just a "hackle" . . .'

'Heckle,' Lambert corrects her (he is certain now that she is doing this on purpose), 'a hackle is the ridge of fur running along the centre of an animal's spine that bristles when it's angry or fearful.'

He leans back and, for comic effect, inspects her, quizzically, from behind.

'It wasn't a heckle,' she repeats (completely ignoring his lame Dad Joke), 'it was an "Interruption". It wasn't an attack, it was a sincere comment; a statement. An *art* statement. It wasn't meant to disrupt so much as to "call forth a shift in perception" . . .'

Lambert blinks. He presumes that India is now quoting from some ridiculously highfalutin cultural studies article . . .

Woah. India? A cultural studies article?!

'It was about honesty,' India continues, 'about *being* honest. And that's why I bunked off today – because I wanted to discover more. I'm interested to learn more. You might not get it – you and Mallory – but I've started something huge. I've started a . . . a movement. And I have a responsibility, which

I take very seriously, to investigate this stuff for my quarter of a million followers.'

'For starters,' Lambert props himself against the arm of the sofa, 'the very fact that you described what a heckle *isn't* means that you understand perfectly well what a heckle *is* . . .'

India emits a frustrated groan and pulls her hood up to the max so that even her single eye is now obscured.

'. . . and correct me if I'm wrong, but as far as *duty* or *responsibility* go, weren't you just filming your own extremely bored response to the gig when TonyInterruptor stood up behind you? I mean we're hardly in Megan Twohey and Jodi Kantor territory here . . .'

Lambert peers intently at his daughter, unsure if she actually knows who Megan Twohey and Jodi Kantor *are* (for the record, India does not know, but she is damned if Lambert Shore should know that she does not know, although she already knows that he knows that she does not know).

'Admittedly,' he runs on, quickly (before she is compelled to embarrass herself with an open admission of ignorance – he is her dad. He loves her), 'you did have the presence of mind to "capture" what happened in order to release it onto your feed, and then sufficient *nous* . . .'

India winces dramatically at Lambert's use of the word 'nous'. For some reason she actively dislikes the word 'nous'.

'. . . sufficient nous to hashtag the venue . . . Although . . .' he shrugs, 'so far as I'm aware, you post everything onto your Stories and hashtag indiscriminately.'

'You *would* say that because you're too old to understand my aesthetic,' India snaps, throwing back her hood, in disgust. Lambert calmly ignores this comment (although there's a measure of truth to it . . . India's *aesthetic*?!).

'If I can just get to my *point* . . .' he doggedly persists.

'Please, God!' India rests her head in her hands despairingly.

'. . . you posted something onto your social media and then somebody else,' he continues, 'someone who *is* in the public eye, decided to co-opt it and to promote it and to throw some – quite frankly – extremely inflammatory behind-the-scenes footage into the mix . . .'

'Is it really so hard to give me a bit of credit?' India interrupts, lifting her eyes from their forensic inspection of the carpet. 'I filmed and then I *edited* something. I realised that it was interesting – that it had value – so I edited it and I promoted it. You act like it's nothing . . .' She forms her hand into a fist and presses it, unconsciously, into the soft leather of the sofa. 'All Mallory ever does is throw shade, and all *you* ever do is defend her. What you don't see – and she doesn't see, either – is that *life* is in the editing. Knowing that something deserves capturing, editing and promoting means using your *judgement*. I used my judgement! You honestly have no confidence in me. You don't think I have any ideas of my own. I have a voice, Dad, and it's *my* voice. I actually have *vision*. I have *intuition*. I have *style*.'

'I do give you credit!' (Lambert is momentarily shaken by the terrible accuracy of India's critique.) 'And I'm not just Mallory's lapdog; that's an extremely insulting thing to imply – and also, coincidentally, not remotely true. I was immensely impressed by what you did with the footage . . .' (I *am* a dick, he thinks).

'Fine. Okay. Great.' India soberly addresses the invisible (and highly supportive/discerning) jury that automatically accompanies all self-righteous teens on their daily perambulations, '. . . So Dad is actually *impressed* that I filmed, edited and posted something online which has earned over 1.6 *million* likes in just over 24 hours. OMFG! Dad is proud!'

India (now definitely on a roll) addresses Lambert directly: 'Cut my allowance for bunking off school today. Force me to do three thousand sit-ups. I'm not fussed. Just please, *please* don't make me listen to another boring lecture on the perils of . . .'

'There's no lecture,' Lambert is, in turn, indignant (mainly because he doesn't have the invisible – and highly supportive/discerning – jury on hand for moral backup). 'And so far as I am aware you don't actually *get* an allowance – unless Mallory is giving you an allowance and hasn't told me about it, in which case, yes, I will be forced to withdraw your allowance . . .'

India rolls her eyes. Haha. Dad is *so* hilarious!

'I'm simply making a point about intellectual property,' he struggles on, manfully, 'about privacy, permission and who owns or controls content . . .'

'Just because your generation is obsessed by "owning" things, by . . . by . . .'

India throws out a hand contemptuously.

'... By protecting or acknowledging the person – or people – who did or said or made something originally?' Lambert chuckles, dryly. 'You're right. We *are* obsessed by it because, oh, I don't know, it's kind of important ...'

India finds her father especially maddening in this moment, and is uncertain whether it's because he's right or because he's extremely smug and stupid. The jury is out (some are now gazing down at their phones with slightly glazed expressions, even though their phones were confiscated at the start of jury duty).

'Kids today don't look at content in the same way your generation did,' India explains. 'For us it's just a kind of ... of ...'

She twirls her hand descriptively.

'Evolution?' Lambert volunteers.

'Like a pick 'n' mix counter at the cinema. Because we're social animals by ...'

Another hand twirl.

'Design?'

'Nature. And knowledge is just a series of ...'

'Pointless memes?'

'*Nothing* is truly original!' she huffs. '*Everything* comes from something or somewhere else! *Everything*. So to try and own a thing, to try and box in a thing or a picture or a thought like it's some kind of ... of *building*?'

She gazes at her architect father, disgusted. 'Not even a building, a bank vault in which everything of value is locked away ...'

'A bank *is* a building,' Lambert avers.

'It's *wrong*!' India ignores him. 'It's greedy and it's wrong. Kids are into sharing and expanding. You know: like the universe. The universe is infinite. But your generation is into guarding and owning; protecting, monitoring, policing ... Ours is a totally different vibe. A different dynamic. A fresh dynamic.'

'I know it's boring and inconvenient,' Lambert sighs, 'but in architecture as in life – and even in the world of social media – there's always a beginning, a foundation, a corner-stone, an origin, an originator ...' Lambert frowns, 'and there's always a price. Someone generally has to pay a price. They make an investment – of thought or money or reputation or privacy or time or energy ... you name it. When you choose to ignore this, then you're automatically inhabiting a position of either entitlement and privilege or – possibly worse still – a position of ... of indolence ... of intellectual negligence ... of ...'

'Inculpability!'

This word is shouted through the open doorway by Mallory as she sweeps past on the way to her study.

India's jaw drops. She lifts her hands at her dad in a '*My God – NOW do you get it?!*' gesture.

Lambert tips his head slightly, in acknowledgement of India's indignation, then pointedly ignores Mallory's interjection (although it's a good word – a perfect word).

'... a position of ... of ...' he repeats, stuttering, '*neurotic innocence ...*'

He finally settles on a satisfactory concept and feels a

momentary sense of relief: '... just a complete refusal to take responsibility. Because someone always has to pay the piper, India. He – or she, or they – *will* be paid. Trust me on that. Nothing comes for free. Someone has to plant the original seed. And you don't always know who that person is, or why they planted it. But everything starts somewhere. Not that they – this person, this same person – necessarily gets to harvest the ... you know ... the ... the fully grown ... marrow ...'

India turns and stares at him, eyebrows raised.

(Okay. Yes. That image *was* possibly, inadvertently, a tiny bit phallic.)

'Like bitcoin,' Lambert staggers on.

'Argh. Not bitcoin *again*,' India mock-hair-tears.

'Bitcoin was intended to offer an alternative to the established ... the traditional financial systems,' Lambert persists, 'but at the end of the day it's all just capitalism; capitalism wearing a different-style coat and a different-style hat, maybe, but still capitalism; an apparently new structure, but involving equivalent levels of opportunism and exploitation ...'

'It's how you *frame* it, Dad,' India interrupts. 'You have an old way of framing things and you are stuck inside that frame ...'

India outlines a large square frame with a dramatic sweep of her arm, 'You can't understand how *we* see things because the old frame is really heavy and hard to move around. Have you ever seen the cartoon where a man is stuck in jail – his hands are holding onto his prison bars and he's staring out from between them, but in actual fact he isn't trapped? There's only one wall! He's free! But because he's staring out through the bars he somehow believes in this . . . this *frame* . . .'

'I've seen the cartoon,' Lambert interrupts. 'It's possible – in fact it's highly probable – that it was me who showed it to you in the first place, which is kind of my point . . .'

'Yes, yes, yes.' India eye-rolls.

'If you've actually been paying attention, you'll have noticed that posting the footage you filmed online has had a whole series of negative consequences for the people *in* the footage. Fi Kinebuchi and Sasha Keyes have both become the focus of hate campaigns. Sasha Keyes and Simo Treen are at loggerheads over the hashtag. Who can even guess how TonyInterruptor feels about the whole thing? I mean to go from relative obscurity to this high level of exposure, overnight? Without ever providing your official consent . . .? *Real lives* are caught up in this now, India; lives and careers. There are causes and effects. There are consequences.'

India seems unmoved by her father's diatribe. She distractedly pulls a loose strand of cotton from the side-stitching of her trousers. 'Simo Treen filmed and then posted the backstage content,' she mutters, carelessly dropping the offending strand onto the carpet, 'I had no control over his decision to do that. And if Sasha Keyes chose to behave like a pig backstage to his co-band member, then surely that's *his* bad?'

'Mallory has been fielding calls from Sasha Keyes's manager all day,' Lambert explains, 'so I imagine that's not exactly how *he's* seeing things currently . . .'

'She's actually had the time to field calls?' India glances up, faux-astonished. 'Even while she was tracking my phone and trailing me around town like a *complete freak*?'

'Mallory wasn't tracking your phone,' he corrects her, 'Jamie Hind's mother saw you hanging around outside the library when she popped in to take him some lunch. Apparently he's on work experience? I'm presuming he messaged you when TonyInterruptor made an appearance . . .?'

'Dad?' India promptly changes the subject. 'Why did I hear you and Mallory arguing about hair earlier?'

'Sorry?' Lambert blinks.

'*Hair*. This weird argument about hair . . .'

'Uh . . . I don't . . .' Lambert winces. 'We weren't arguing.'

His phone pings. He glances down at it distractedly, looks up, then glances back down again, surprised.

'Yes, you were!' India insists.

'No. Not at all.' He looks up again. 'It was just an animated discussion. Anyway, we're not talking about that right now, India, we're . . .'

'Who just messaged you?' India demands (her instinct for adult hubris/hypocrisy is infallible). 'What's wrong?'

'Nobody messaged me,' Lambert protests. 'Nothing's wrong.'

'Dad . . .' India shuffles speedily across the sofa, closer to where Lambert is leaning, grabs his arm and pulls him down next to her. She lowers her voice conspiratorially. 'What's the real deal with Mallory and her hair?'

'The real deal? How d'you mean? There *is* no deal.'

Lambert talks at normal volume to signpost that there isn't a problem. 'We weren't arguing. Mallory was just . . . just . . . she was just teasing me about something, that's all.'

Lambert's phone pings again. 'It was just a casual conversation,' he continues, 'nothing to . . .' He is looking down at his phone, '. . . nothing to stress about.'

India is also now peering down at the screen on Lambert's phone.

'*Fi?*' she murmurs. 'Is that from Fi? Dad? Why is Fi Kinebuchi sending you the address of a London hair salon?'

'Oh . . . Is she?' Lambert pretends innocence.

'So it's true?' India is disconcerted. "Mallory is pissed because you're secretly making some kind of . . . of *video* installation . . . about *hair*?!'

'No . . . no . . .' Lambert shifts in his seat. 'This whole thing is just a . . .'

'Isn't it weird that you should receive a message on your phone from Fi Kinebuchi about a hair salon in London at the *exact same moment* we are having a conversation in which you hotly deny any interest in doing a video installation about hair?' India demands. 'This is . . .'

She twirls her hand.

'Unexpected?' he volunteers.

'No. Peculiar,' she pauses, 'Oh. Or is Fi Kinebuchi in the habit of messaging you all the time?'

'Um . . .'

'Wow. That's so . . . I dunno . . .' India grabs a cushion from the sofa and clasps it in front of her like it's a temporary buffer against her father's bullshit. 'That's like . . .' she ponders, '. . . so disturbing!'

'Fi has never messaged me before,' Lambert insists, and in all sincerity, 'I didn't even know she had my number. I've no idea where she got it from. Possibly the office at work. I had a brief conversation with her in the staffroom earlier about J. D. Salinger, and Jane Finch happened to be walking by . . . She's friends with Mallory, so I imagine . . .'

'Mallory is like the friggin' Stasi!' India exclaims. She is only half-serious. She is also half-serious.

'And yet *you're* the one reading my messages and sneaking around the house listening to private . . .?'

'I just wanted a glass of water!' India is affronted. 'I went to the kitchen to get myself one, but you and Mallory were already in there arguing about hair. And now Fi Kinebuchi is messaging you, out of the blue, and sending you the address of a London *hair* salon . . .'

Lambert opens his mouth to respond, then closes it again.

'Why, though?' India wonders. 'What *is* this thing about hair?' She suddenly lowers her voice again. 'And why does Mallory get to decide how you choose to express yourself creatively?'

'Okay. Okay . . . So hair . . . hair is just a . . . just a "side-bar",' Lambert brackets the concept of 'hair' with both of his hands, 'and Mallory *doesn't* get to decide. Although I have a great deal of respect for Mallory's opinions, in much the same way that I have a great admiration for your judgement and editing . . .'

India eyes her father with a cool, assessing gaze. A beat passes.

'Are we being honest here?' she wonders.

'Oh God,' Lambert groans.

'Did Mallory get miffed because you've been messaging Fi Kinebuchi in secret? Or was it because you didn't tell her you were making a video installation together? Was it because she didn't know, and she likes to know about *everything* you're doing – and everything *I'm* doing – because she's so incredibly opinionated and controlling? Or was it about the hair? Because Mallory shaved hers off when Gunn was born?'

'Um . . .' Lambert is floored.

His phone pings. It is Fi Kinebuchi, again.

India sees this, even before he does.

'Fi Kinebuchi, *AGAIN?!*'

She uncurls her arms from around the cushion and presents it to him as if the cushion is now a physical representation of her confusion, her disgust, her tragic loss of innocence. He accepts the cushion. (Why am I just passively accepting this symbolic cushion and all that it seemingly implies? he thinks.)

India stands up. She takes out her own phone. She expertly angles it and commences filming herself. 'This is a shitshow, Dad,' she murmurs into the phone (including him in the shot), 'just a shitshow,' she adds, and then: 'If you have anything meaningful or *honest* you'd like to say to me on this issue, then you can find me in my room.'

She walks to the door, still filming, her posture – her

carriage – full of a kind of implicit disgruntlement . . . no . . . disappointment . . . no . . . exasperation.

Lambert struggles to understand how a conversation about India bunking off school has now become a vehicle (an out-of-control school bus) for her public disillusionment with *his* behaviour.

'*Hair?!*' India mutters (apparently to the door handle). 'So weird!'

'Are you intending to share this jewel with your 250,000 followers?' Lambert calls after her. No response. He is just wondering whether to make a last-ditch attempt to reclaim some tattered remnant of parental authority by taking her to task for her earlier foul language, when . . .

Ping!

(His phone.)

'GAH!'

(From the hallway.)

Okay, he thinks, glancing down and rapidly turning his device to silent; might need to let that one go. Just this once.

8

In a quiet moment (and, let's face it, there aren't many quiet moments in the full-bore life of Mallory Shore) she sits at her desk in her 'office' (their rambling old home's former larder) pretending to do some work and struggling to remember what it was exactly that TonyInterruptor *said* to infuriate her so thoroughly during their brief encounter. What was it?

What was it that he *said*?

To infuriate her?

So thoroughly?

Mallory attempts to break it down . . .

Oh my.

Nothing materialises.

Absolutely nothing.

Thin air.

A quiet, empty pulsing.

Her mind briefly returns to an earlier conversation in the

kitchen with Lambert about a purported new 'art' project he's secretly been planning.

Seriously, though?!
Lambert?!
Secret *art* project?!
How the . . .?
I mean . . . I mean . . .
Her blood instantly starts to boil.

The secrecy! *WHY?*
And then (worse still) to find out about this whole thing – this . . . this ridiculous . . . preposterous . . . creepily sensual . . . objectifying . . . borderline-predatory idea – via *Jane Finch* of all people? JANE FINCH! Sworn frenemy! To have to . . . to fudge her reaction like that in the toothpaste aisle at Tesco Metro?

(Damn! I forgot the cotton wool balls! Damn! *Damn!*)

'Oh! Yes! You mean . . . um . . . *that* . . . um . . . *hair* thing? Of course! The thing about . . . um . . . about *hair* . . .?'
(Mallory imagines herself raising an unconscious hand to her own shorn head as the conversation awkwardly unfolds. Urgh. *Agony!*)

He's always had an embarrassing crush on Fi Kinebuchi. Fact.

He pretends to be an ardent fan of Sasha Keyes, but there's never been any doubt about who he's really attending all those live performances to gawp at . . .

Grrrr!

Mallory leans forward and types PRICK PRICK PRICK PRICK into her legal document. She leans back and inspects this, with some vague sense of satisfaction. She inhales deeply. She exhales. She leans forward and deletes it again.

Okay . . . His voice, maybe? The tone of TonyInterruptor's voice? Was that it?

She rests her weight on her elbows and her chin on both fists. She struggles to remember it . . . TonyInterruptor's voice. The actual . . . the natural tone of it. Was it supercilious? Was it sharp? Was it patronising? She tries to remember his voice (the accent, the inflections, the timbre), but all that readily springs to mind is a powerful visual image of his hands, which are holding a roll-up in that particular, somehow-evocative way (huh? Why 'somehow-evocative'?! Why?), with the end – the filter? – pinched between first finger and thumb, then the burning tip pointed in towards the palm. So the cigarette itself is unseen. Curls of smoke glide through the various gaps and angles of the hand.

Mallory pauses in delighted remembrance of this gentle gliding. Then, moments later, she recoils at the thought of how smoky the skin on his hand must smell because of it.

Seriously, though? She snorts. Has it come to this? Sitting at my desk, trying to work, refusing to think about Lambert's embarrassing crush on Fi Kinebuchi (which has now been squeezed, moulded and extrapolated into some completely unexpected and vaguely unsettling ART project), while *actually* deeply engrossed in imagining the smell of TonyInterruptor's cupped palm? Ridiculous! Bizarre! Depraved!

Mallory forces her attention back onto her laptop and the legal document she's copy-editing.

Fi Kinebuchi is such a cliché. A living cliché! Such a mousy, beige, obliging 'facilitator'! This fusty, amiable, passive CONDUIT for the male creative ego. Just the way ... the way she sits there, smiling moronically (in the film footage), as Sasha Keyes belittles her! Is it *really* sincere? The Buddha act? Can she *really* be so airy? So intellectual? So submissive? So vague? So vanilla?

The door creaks a little. Gunn sidles into the office and stands quietly behind her mother's chair. Mallory says nothing. She continues to 'concentrate' on what she's doing (Gunn needs to respect that fact that her mother has a whole other life outside of the infinite domestic drudgery of the home, aka the infinite professional drudgery of 'work'. She is, *ahem*, BUSY).

Gunn *is* respectful (if silence is respectful), but she is also determinedly scratching away at something.

Mallory grimaces but she doesn't turn to look. She simply intuits that Gunn is scratching at her head; at her dreadlocks. Gunn wears dreadlocks because she has never permitted either parent to brush her hair. She is hyper-sensitive to touch.

For this same reason she also refuses to wear shoes (just occasionally Crocs with socks on the very worst days of winter).

Oh for heaven's sake! Mallory thinks. Is it lice again?

Lice are a plague to children's dreadlocks because the hair cannot be combed. Although the dreadlocks aren't really at fault, Mallory reasons, because the hair couldn't have been combed even before there were dreadlocks in it . . .

Okay. Um.

Her eyes defocus and she briefly returns to her illicit ruminations.

(The cigarette . . .

The hand . . .

The curl of smoke . . .)

I mean the IRONY that Lambert should be considering an ART project in which hair (HAIR!) is the main component? When Mallory (HIS WIFE) has *no* hair, and Gunn (HIS CHILD) has *huge* hair issues?!

Just . . . just . . .

Insensitive! Unbelievably insensitive!

HAIR?!

Of *all* subjects?!

It's just *SO* CONTENTIOUS! SO *INCREDIBLY* CONTENTIOUS!!

Scratch scratch scratch . . .

TonyInterruptor suddenly stands before her.

But *shouldn't* art be contentious? he demands.
Mallory is riled.
What?!
Sorry . . . ART . . . He grins, Shouldn't ART be contentious?

Mallory's stomach contracts. *What do you mean?!* she snaps. Well shouldn't ART be an exploration? A new way of looking/seeing? A re-evaluation? A 'working-through?' He smirks. Mallory gazes at this imagined, smirking TonyInterruptor, absolutely outraged.

HE'S SO FUCKING SMUG!

Do you (Mallory) somehow OWN the concept of hair, now? he asks.

Scratch scratch scratch . . .

Mallory clears her mind in much the same way a child might clear the grey screen of an Etch A Sketch (by flipping it over, decisively).
Flip.
Clear screen.

'Is your head itching, Gunn?'
No response.

Scratch scratch scratch . . .

*

Mallory re-enters the vaults of her memory from a different angle. An explorer in an unknown land . . .
She imagines Neil Armstrong's first steps on the moon (big, bouncy spacesuit.
Poff . . . poff . . . poff . . .).

What does she find?

Hmm. There are some random-seeming sense-memories of TonyInterruptor's (I *can't* keep on calling him that. I *can't*. It feels . . . stupid. It feels . . . *less*. What *is* his name? What *is* his real name?) green eyes (hazel eyes . . . green eyes) and the closeness of his shave. A grey-bluey-closeness. On his jaw.

He *did* actually look a bit like Anders Danielsen Lie! Arrogant. No. Haughty. Sensitive. In just the same way that Anders Danielsen Lie is haughty and sensitive. Brooding. Thoughtful (dreamy).

Mallory saves the document on her laptop, shrinks it, and googles Anders Danielsen Lie.
Why am I doing this?
Complete waste of time!

She gazes at a collection of images of Anders Danielsen Lie. Hmm. Yes. They *do* look similar. And yet . . .

Scratch scratch scratch . . .

'Coconut oil?' she asks, without turning from her screen. 'Would that relieve it?'

'Huh?'

(Gunn is now sitting, cross-legged, on the tiled floor behind her chair.)

'The itching. That tiled floor is *very* cold.'

No response.

Mallory returns to her google search and quickly finds herself reading an article in *Vanity Fair*.

Good heavens. That's amazing. Anders Danielsen Lie is *a doctor*. In real life! How intriguing. A doctor!

Ooh. Well that was definitely unexpected . . .

Scratch scratch scratch . . .

'Go and fetch some coconut oil,' Mallory suggests. 'You know where it is. The cupboard under the sink in the big bathroom. The glass jar with the blue label. If you go and get it then I'll . . .'

Mallory imagines Anders Danielsen Lie as a doctor. He is now playing the part of a doctor in the film of Anders Danielsen Lie's life, which is currently screening, unedited, at the little cinema inside her head. She wonders – briefly – if it's possible for Anders Danielsen Lie to live an actual, normal life without being inexplicably (because she hasn't worked out all the details, yet) trapped inside the 'performance' of a life.

Curious thought. No. Stupid thought.

*

I'm the person trapped inside the performance of a life, Mallory sighs. That's *me*. That's not Anders Danielsen Lie. That's *me*.

ART PROJECT?
ABOUT *HAIR?!*

Urgh. Stop it. Just stop it with the raging. Just stop it with the obsessing. This isn't helping.
Okay. Back to . . .

Mallory finds herself imagining having some kind of an accident while on holiday in Norway and being taken (by ambulance) to Anders Danielsen Lie's hospital. She is carried into casualty on a stretcher. Okay. So what exactly is wrong with her? How is she injured? No blood. God, no. Nothing too unsightly. A twisted ankle! It may be broken. It isn't broken (thankfully), but Anders Danielsen Lie (he is wearing green hospital scrubs) will need to manipulate said ankle, with infinite care, in order to discover, definitively, that the ankle isn't broken.

Gunn still hasn't moved. She is no longer scratching. She has taken a hole punch from a drawer in Mallory's desk (the drawer has been left open) and she is now applying the punch to a piece of paper.

Oh. Hang on . . . Mallory frowns. What about Lambert, though? Where precisely is Lambert during this whole ankle-twisting fantasy?
She definitely doesn't want Lambert taking up any unnecessary space inside her erotic hospital dreamscape.

Where *is* Lambert, though?
She smiles to herself, wryly.
But of course! He is filming his secret ART project about HAIR!!

The dick.

No. Stop it.
Um. Lambert is looking after the girls. Naturally. He has taken them back to the hotel, even though he is still deeply concerned about her (Mallory) because . . . well . . . she has somehow hurt her ankle and she is at a hospital in Norway on her own, and Lambert is a nice person who cares about people.

Mallory scowls. This doesn't feel good. This doesn't feel . . . um . . . sexy.
Sexy?!
Mallory winces.
Okay, no. No. She has gone on a solo trip to Norway because of . . . because of work. Lambert is at home, in England, looking after the girls. Although . . . well, it's difficult to imagine this scenario because Mallory cannot trust anyone to take care of Gunn except her. Not even Lambert.
(Mallory feels a sharp jab of both pride and pure irritation at this detail.)

Right. Okay. So there is *no* real chance of being in Norway for work and suddenly twisting an ankle. (How did she twist her ankle? On a running machine in the hotel? On a hike?

Does her holiday insurance even cover a visit to the hospital?)
Mallory googles: health service, Norway.
She discovers that Norway has a good State Healthcare System which isn't entirely free to all citizens/visitors but requires financial contributions. She clicks on the *People Ask* link: *does Norway have a good Health Service?* and discovers that they rank number 12 in the World Index of Healthcare Innovation . . .
The what?
No.
Stop this.
I hate this.
Fucking admin. Even in my fantasies. Fucking admin.
Why can't I simply enjoy an idle fantasy without the interference of admin?

Is this what it's come to?

Also . . .
Am I having a relatively innocent erotic fantasy about Anders Danielsen Lie, or . . . or is Anders Danielsen Lie simply a clumsy cover – a surrogate – for TonyInterruptor?

Am I actually sitting here, pretending to work, with *my child* sitting on the floor directly behind me (applying a hole punch to what may possibly be an important legal document), and fantasising about TonyInterruptor in the guise of Anders Danielsen Lie?

What a truly demoralising scenario.

Mallory returns to the *Vanity Fair* article.
Oh. Ha! Look at that . . . Anders Danielsen Lie has *two* daughters with his MODEL wife . . . !
Mallory is crushed.
A *model.* Hospital doctor/actor marries *model.*

Mallory now googles: Anders Danielsen Lie wife.
What?! She gapes. So incredibly beautiful! A ridiculously beautiful blonde model:
Is-e-lin Steiro.

Although . . . *hmm* . . . she attended . . . she attended the Oslo School of Architecture and Design (!! room for a whole separate fantasy involving Lambert and Is-a-lin? Is-*e*-lin here . . .). And . . . Okay . . . She had a role in *Oslo, August 31st.* Great film. Immensely powerful film . . . Mallory nods gravely to herself at the memory of the film. She has great recall on the film. Evocative and disturbing film. Important film. Deeply traumatic film.

So surely that must've been how they . . .?
Nope. Film released 2011. Met 2007. Married 2008.

Uh, maybe it works, though?
Four years to turn the film around? Is that typical?

Although, on a purely pragmatic level: why would Anders Danielsen Lie want to flirt with (or be irresistibly attracted to) Mallory, when he has two adorable daughters and is married to a stupidly gorgeous model?
Seems improbable.

And why would Mallory (who also has two daughters – neither especially adorable – and is married to

Lambert) want to flirt (or be irresistibly attracted to) Anders Danielsen Lie?

Um.

Although this *isn't* Anders Danielsen Lie, is it? This is TonyInterruptor with his awful attention-seeking antics at provincial gigs and his vile, smoky hand.

Yup.

Mallory sighs. Her Anders Danielsen Lie fantasy has been ruined by a combination of real facts and fantasy admin. Urgh. There's nothing workably erotic to collapse into now. Everything is tarnished. By obsessive thinking. By excessive fantasy organisation. It's too weird. And it's infuriating.

How noble, though: to be a doctor. Like Chekhov. To be a doctor *and* an artist, like Chekhov.

Please stop thinking about Anders Danielsen Lie and his model wife. This is a dreadful waste of time. It's silly. It's insincere.

Is this *honest?* Are we all being *honest* here? You, especially?

FFS!

TonyInterruptor (in this new fantasy) points an accusatory finger (supported by an offensively smoky palm) directly at Mallory.

Mallory scowls.

Is TonyInterruptor a real person *and* an actor, too?

Hmm. That's an authentically interesting thought.

Actually, no.

That's not a remotely interesting thought. In fact it's an incredibly stupid thought: the idle and fundamentally pointless thought of a provincial housewife/lawyer who no longer has any – not ANY – connection to her sensual self.
None.

Mallory twists around on her chair.
'What exactly are you hole-punching there, Gunn? Did you check that it wasn't an important document?'

Gunn doesn't answer. (How might Gunn possibly be expected to delineate between a so-called 'important' document and an apparently 'insignificant' document? How? She has the comprehension skills of a three-year-old.)

Gunn has removed the plastic base of the metal hole punch (where the little circles of paper are stored, post-punching) and has scattered them onto the tiled floor where she is forming a design out of them in the manner of Yayoi Kusama. Lambert had persuaded Mallory to take Gunn to the big exhibition of Kusama's work at the Tate Modern because he felt, intuitively, that Gunn would find the . . . And he was right. Lambert is invariably right. Lambert's intuition is invariably . . .
She had loved it.

His voice? TonyInterruptor's voice? The *actual words* he spoke . . .?

Mallory can now only imagine the voice of Anders Danielsen Lie. In *Reprise*; in the film *Reprise.*

So pretentious. But excellent. Great soundtrack. Remember . . .

um . . . she googles . . . ah . . . Espen Klouman Høiner? So handsome! Too handsome.

Do all Norwegian men have three names?

Espen?

That's cute.

Espen.

Like the tree.

Aspen.

Yes . . . Anders DL has a slightly nasal voice, doesn't he? (Mallory watches the trailer for *Reprise* on mute.) ADL is speaking, confidently, but with his trademark sullen vulnerability, in Norwegian (*Duh*). There's a sense that his voice is reverberating from the top of his palate. (Mallory is not a speech therapist – obviously – and has no idea really where or how a voice might be expected to reverberate.)

What an excellent trailer! It gives her goosebumps. Even on mute.

*Re*prise. Why that italicised font on the first two letters?

*Re*prise?

Argh! This is a blind alley! Just stop it with all the pointless researching of Anders Danielsen Lie! Why are you obsessing over Anders Danielsen Lie when you are actually trying to think about TonyInterruptor?

Huh?

Um. Well, possibly . . . Mallory promptly answers herself . . . because they are both, at some level, made up. They are just ideas.

Or just feelings *about* ideas.
Her feelings about ideas.
That's it.
But then aren't all people 'just ideas'? Or just feelings about ideas? Isn't Gunn 'just ideas'? Aren't I (Mallory Shore) 'just ideas'?

Mallory grabs her phone, heads to her Instagram and searches for TonyInterruptor. She watches the footage.

HOW MANY VIEWS?!?!
Complete madness!

She listens to his voice with her phone held up close to her ear (*very quietly*). The sound of his voice is compromised. Definitely compromised (well, she presumes that it is compromised because it's low-quality footage – and *very quiet* – and there's the sound of music in the background etc. . . .)

But in person, though? Did he sound different in person? In real life?

Hmm.
She concentrates.
Nothing.
Nothing manifests.
Okay.

If she really, really focuses her mind, might she be able to replay the entire conversation back, word for word? Exchange by exchange? That whole conversation from outside of the library?

She tries.

Hang on . . .

Is this a '*re*prise'?

Am I '*re*prising' the conversation?

Mallory googles 'reprise meaning'.

A repeated passage in music.

Repeat.

Wow.

Why does that give me a funny feeling?

A significant feeling?

She sighs.

This is ludicrous. I'm like a white mouse in a science experiment, running frantically through some kind of . . . of . . . well-lit maze. Slightly panicked. Constructing meaning. Desperately trying to figure my way out.

Oh. And failing.

*Re*prise.

Stop it.

The exchange outside of the library . . .

Think.

Mallory closes her eyes, waits for a moment, and then her body is suddenly flooded by a succession of powerful sense-memories. Ambient sensations. Beautiful sensations. Like the warm wind against the skin on the side of her neck. And ... ooh ... a smell of some kind of ... what was it? She frowns. *Mmm.* Red pepper. Cumin. Mint. Sumak. Turkish spices from a nearby ...

Oh yes. And the sun. A patch of light. He was sitting in a patch of light and his chin was lifted. His eyes were closed. The cigarette ...
She shudders.

Wow.
Wow.
Who knew that this particular moment was so resonant with ... with ...?
What?
Pleasure?
Sensation?
Feelings about ideas?
No.
Emotion?
Stuff?

Wow!
Mallory is vaguely unsettled by this. She is confounded.

So much subtle feeling. Beneath all the fury and the irritation.

*

HIS VOICE?
Her eyes ping open.
Remember?!
His *voice*?!
Isn't that the whole point of this?
To remember?

Hang on a second . . .
She scowls.
Am I just confusing that moment – that, yes, admittedly deeply ambient moment – with the left-over sensibilities of the creative vision of Joachim Trier? With that evocative film trailer?

Were those *real* feelings?
Aren't they *rogue* feelings?

Joachim Trier is such a wonderful director.
Is Joachim Trier related to Lars von . . .?
No.

Are those *my* ambient feelings, or am I just borrowing (or clumsily superimposing) the . . .?

HIS VOICE!
TONYINTERRUPTOR'S VOICE!
CONCENTRATE!

*

She finds it difficult to conjure. No matter how hard she tries. There's a kind of . . . um . . . a blockage. An odd feeling. An unsettled feeling. Almost . . . I don't know . . . it's confusing. Initially there's a sense of . . . of irritation and surprise followed by a sharp pang of indignation followed by . . .? Well, more indignation. I mean the smugness! The unalloyed smugness! His expression! The way he inhaled on his cigarette, so casually and apparently unconcerned, *in the presence of a young child*!

Honestly!

And then . . . I don't know . . .

What is that?!

In her chest . . .? In her belly?

A curling . . . a writhing . . .

Embarrassment?!

Why?

Why embarrassment?

Oooh. And it's not a particularly good feeling, is it? A sort of slight and then gradually strengthening prickling and burning sensation beneath her diaphragm – or the upper regions of her belly – which hurts a little, to begin with, in an . . . an emotional way. It's an almost . . . an almost cringey feeling . . .

Mallory hates this feeling.

Humiliation.

Oh Lord! Did he actually even SAY anything?!!

(She's always known the answer to this question. The answer to this question is a definitive 'no'.)

Did he actually even *say* anything?!

Surely . . .?

But that makes no sense! For the person who – in her mind, and in the world of 'social media' – is defined by speaking out, by interrupting . . . for this same person not to even open his mouth during an encounter (a slightly combative exchange – although not truly an 'exchange', apparently) but to . . . to sit calmly and quietly and simply hold his counsel? Impossible!

Unless . . .?

Was it her? Did she (Mallory) just bombard him with words and opinions and accusations and preconceptions so that there was simply no . . . no opportunity? No chance to speak?

Oh *shit*.

Surely not?

His voice?

He must've said *something*?!

Because if he didn't say anything. If he didn't speak. If he held his counsel. If he chose to hold his counsel, then surely that would make him . . .

THE WINNER?

Surely that would make him . . .

TRIUMPHANT?

*

And where was she . . .? Wittering on? Chuntering on? Lost in her own little suburban – provincial – dramas to the point that . . . So he didn't really get an opportunity to . . .? To defend himself? To answer? To say anything?

Please, no.
Anything but that!

Oh Lord! To've been so enraged and preoccupied and idiotic and unguarded in front of *this* man!
This man!
Of *all* men!
To've been so pompous and self-involved and strident and opinionated in front of *this* man!
This man!

She can't think about it.
Too painful!

And also:
Who the fuck do I think I am?
(The shame!)
What gives me the right?
(The embarrassment!)
To behave like this?
(The humiliation!)
Accusing a teenage girl of behaving like a teenage girl when I, myself, am behaving exactly like a teenage girl?

(The mortification!)
A teenage girl but with all the tools and the experience and the responsibilities of womanhood?

Urgh. The hypocrisy!

Mallory's cheeks gently burn. They sizzle. They glow.

Etch A Sketch.
Flip.

Um.
Which was it? Did he refuse to engage? Or did she simply bombard him?
Which was it?
Could it be both?

This suddenly matters enormously: did he choose to hold his counsel? Or did he simply miss his opportunity to react (to respond)?

Calculated?
versus
Bullied?

Um. She doesn't know. She suspects it's the former. And this is irritating to her because, well, if he *is* TonyInterruptor then surely the whole point of him, the whole reason for him (to exist, to be) is that he interrupts things? He is An Interruptor.

But when she thinks of their brief encounter, she realises that he is more than that – more complicated. More nuanced. More . . . more . . . human.

Human.

He is experience and memory and sensation and feeling and prejudice and idealism and hope and woundedness. A mess of things.
Human.
Just like her.

Why did I attack him? she wonders.
Where is my justification?

Because of how Lambert reported their conversation, post-gig? Is it Lambert's fault, then? (Please let it be Lambert's fault!) That refusal to shake his hand which seemed . . . it seemed arrogant.
(Is it so wrong to refuse to shake a person's hand?
Is it really so wrong?)
Although he *did* shake Lambert's hand. He just hesitated before shaking it. That's all.

What's the matter with me? she wonders. Isn't India right?
'YOU ARE NOT MY JUDGE AND JURY.'
Remember?

*

Why this need to be so absolute? So precise? About everything? To come down, so definitively, on either one side or the other? To be so comprehensive.
Like car insurance.

She shudders.
What a stupid thing.
How *stupid*.
What a truly shallow and unsophisticated response to the inconsistent, endlessly variable, fundamentally unreadable and unpredictable shitstorm that is life!

Mallory's stomach contracts.

Why is this happening? Why this overwhelming feeling?

What is it about this man?!

To stand up and say something?
To sit down and say nothing?
And for these two acts to seem – to feel – so devastating. To her? To Mallory Shore? Who is perched at her desk in her tiny larder/office in her large suburban home in this hateful – *hateful* – cathedral town?

I can't . . .
Can't think . . .
Too painful.

Just have to keep . . .
Charging on.
Because if I don't . . .
If I don't . . .
If I stop . . .
If I stop and actually . . . actually *think* . . . actually *process* . . .

Gunn scratches.

Coconut oil!

Mallory slams down the lid of her laptop, springs to her feet, and – because she can't shove back her chair (as Gunn is there) – launches herself sideways. But the drawer is still open. She is wearing her long denim smock. She topples over the drawer. She yells as she falls. She twists. She hits a bookshelf. She sees her newish copy of Adélia Prado's *The Mystical Rose* as she collapses and idly thinks: I still haven't read that. I really must read that. Alongside it, an early edition of *Moominvalley in November*. Alongside that, a Martin Amis paperback with an unsightly crease along its spine. How did that happen? she wonders, followed by: FUCKING FUCK FUCK FI KINEBUCHI! as she tries, very hard (and with moderate levels of success), not to land, with her whole weight, on top of the child.

9

It's an intensely private life. He exists quietly and unobtrusively, generating a bare minimum of 'ripples'. It's a solitary life and he is unbound. He is untethered. He may wander, but he may also decide to remain entrenched. He is impulsive, but steady. He is measured. He is responsible. And it is this . . . this quiet steadiness, this easy disconnectedness, that grants him his curious sense of liberty, that frees him up to saunter boldly and audaciously into the artificial confines of 'art' and 'film' and 'culture', to gaze at them (frankly, openly), and then to poke out his tongue at them (if he feels the urge), without any hint of sophistry or self-consciousness. Without showiness. Without (at least almost without) compunction . . .

Ohhh, but *who cares?*

*

But who cares *WHY*?

·

India is in her room trying to design stickers. Her initial impulse was to make badges, but after some serious consideration she has decided that a badge demands too much commitment, is too weighted with – *urgh* – 'meaning', and that a sticker is naturally more radical, looser, throwaway, nonchalant . . .

Sprezzatura! This is the special word the Italians devised (which Lambert loves to drop, willy-nilly, into casual conversation) to describe the act of creating something superlative but with no apparent effort. The key word being 'apparent' because there must, inevitably – Lambert informs India, sagely – be immense amounts of effort involved in doing something (anything) extremely well.

'The world,' he explains, 'is basically divided into two kinds of high achiever: the first type will make a *huge show* over how difficult and challenging a project is. They will share every heroic detail. They will enact, minute by minute, how impossible the struggle is. They will demand validation *every inch* of the way. They will expect you to hold your breath and watch them teeter on the edge, the very brink, of disaster, then finally, miraculously, expel that same breath in a shout of triumph as they deliver their company merger (or new invention, or song, or plate of handmade pasta) into the world.

The second type, though? The second type of high achiever? The absolute opposite. They make no fuss at all. They publish no running commentary. They are secretive and calm, much preferring to don the mask of insouciance, to pretend that this same accomplishment (the new invention, the company merger, the prog-rock album about the melting temperature of cheese) amounts to little more than a hill of beans. It's happened almost by magic – effortlessly – through conjuring.

'Oh! Really? The best pasta you've ever eaten? Huh!'

This, Lambert tells his daughter (who probably isn't paying attention), is at the core of what it means to be 'cool' (although 'cool' – even in air quotes – is not a word that is even remotely acceptable to India).

Sprezzatura, she deduces, is, essentially, a pretence of studied indifference, a cynical, surreptitious, passive-aggressive projection of simplicity and ease, secretly underpinned by jaw-dropping levels of exertion and expertise.

'It's like being a swan,' Lambert grins, 'floating on a pond while producing no ripples, a vision of grace and elegance. But underneath? Below the waterline? Conveniently hidden from view? Two giant grey webbed feet paddling away, hell for leather . . .'

Sprezzatura.

Why?

Why do people feel the need to do this?

India ponders this mystery.
Insecurity? Modesty? Arrogance?

Does TonyInterruptor have *Sprezzatura*? Is he actually trying really hard and pretending not to? Is he head or heart? Is he spontaneous or calculating?

This feels important. But also ineffable. Intangible.

And India?
(Qui, *moi?!*)

India never tries too hard, surely? Because she's a girl. Girls are programmed by culture, by nature, not to be too eager or too competitive. It's unladylike. They are simply required to wake up, each day, and be perfectly polished, pristine, placid, coy, obliging, kittenish, unthreatening . . .

Hmm.
India scowls.

Grrr.

Stickers.

Surely stickers are intrinsically more casual, fluid, relaxed, careless, ephemeral (cheaper) than badges and can be more readily attached to the manifold yet fundamentally random artefacts of culture: books, phones, advertising hoardings, items of street furniture, plus *also* to blazer lapels, foreheads, school bags etc.

Stickers are wonderfully democratic. Impermanent and fascinatingly degradable. Inherently 'underground'. Fit for purpose.

Is
this
honest?

Hmm. *Is* this? Honest? Stickers are obviously (India intuits) *way* more honest than badges. Or … or are badges way *too* honest … too eager? Too shout-y? Too train-spotter-y? Too smug? Too prissy? Plus *round*.

Is
This
Honest?

The three words feel harder to place onto a sphere or disc, because the final word is longer … hmm … then the question mark. A spatial nightmare … although … um …

Is this
honest?

… would probably work … uh … but the letters risk being illegibly small …

Oh. Unless you made the badge bigger than the customary 25mm? You could expand to 38mm, even 55mm?

India bursts out laughing. *What?!* Imagine! How excruciating! The 55mm badge! The kind of badge you'd find pinned to the front of a YOU ARE 8 birthday card . . .!

An involuntary shudder brings her cynical yiffles to an abrupt halt.

Oh God. Too awful to contemplate. The 55mm badge. Just too awful.

(For all her indignation/ferocity/denial India is 100% the daughter of a savvy, urban Kentish architecture professor.)

Decision made. Stickers are better. Utterly superior. Although there's still plenty to agonise over . . . Colour. Size. And obviously THE FONT.

Prior to this moment, India had never really given much thought to type/fonts because The Man – i.e. The Forces of International Capitalism (sweet, chocolate, crisp and soft drinks manufacturers – TikTok – Instagram) had already chosen the fonts *for* India. Those decisions had already been made by serried ranks of graphic designers; qualified professionals who (for some weird and inexplicable reason) had dedicated ENERGY and THOUGHT to the creation/selection/choice of all or any particular type.

India glances up for a moment, scowling (uh . . . hang on . . .?). A hand is lifted to one of her earplugs (she is listening to *The*

Dark Side of The Moon). The walls appear to be strobing. Blue lights. What is this? But before she can fully process, another thought strikes her (of equivalent importance) and she jumps up from the rug she's been lolling on, slips out of her room and heads downstairs to poke around in Lambert's study. She is searching for . . .

Red spine? Orange spine?

Ah-ha!

A lovely hardback copy of Simon Garfield's *Just My Type*.

She pulls it out of the bookshelf and holds it in her hand, dedicating a few moments to the feeling of how amazing it is (or how amazing the human brain is – *her* brain) for somehow sensing that this book existed among all the hundreds of other books in Lambert's study (it sits on a shelf directly above his desk at the exact height her eyes love to roam when Lambert is reclining in his chair, expounding confidently, telling her something 'important'). She had noticed it before, as her eyes idly explored various titles, and had paused on it, confused, thinking that perhaps it was a book about . . . um . . . dating? But it wasn't. It isn't.

This particular book has been sitting here, passively, waiting for this moment, in the way only a book really can (enigmatically, contained-ly), until she finally realised – small firework explodes! – that she *cares* about fonts (I CARE ABOUT FONTS! INDIA SHORE CARES ABOUT FONTS!).

Such patience! Aren't books so helpful like that? The way that they just stay quietly contained, on a shelf, hidden between two hard covers, asking nothing, offering nothing, right up until the moment when . . . when . . .

Without the disruption of TonyInterruptor, India Shore may never have connected to the fact (the reality) that she is committed to/cares about fonts. Without the disruption of TonyInterruptor, India Shore may never have realised (a mere three pages into Garfield's book) that certain kinds of specialised knowledge can be interesting – engaging – fun.
Simon Garfield has *Sprezzatura*!
Suddenly it all makes sense.
To work hard at being effortless.
Of course! But *of course!*

Here it comes! Here it comes!
A neural pathway fizzles.
A tiny, revolutionary, shift in consciousness.

It's an intensely private life. He exists quietly and unobtrusively, generating a bare minimum of 'ripples'. It's a solitary life and he is unbound. He is untethered. He may wander, but he may also decide to remain . . .

*

Fi Kinebuchi stops re-reading and checks her phone.
Nothing.
She returns to the copy, *pffts* quietly (I mean *really?* He is 'untethered'?!),
then quickly scrolls down the page to the comments section.
Oh my.
Oh my oh my.

It's an intensely private life . . .

WHAT IS HE CONCEALING?

He exists quietly and unobtrusively . . .

WHO IS HE AVOIDING?

generating a bare minimum of 'ripples' . . .

WHY SO CONSTRAINED?

It's a solitary life . . .

HE IS FRIENDLESS!

and he is unbound . . .

WHO GRANTED HIM HIS FREEDOM?

*

He is untethered . . .

WHO CUT THE ROPE?

He may wander . . .

IRRESPONSIBLE!

. . . but he may also decide to remain entrenched . . .

STUCK!

He is impulsive, but steady . . .

UNPREDICTABLE!

He is measured. He is responsible . . .

DULL!

And it is this . . . this quiet steadiness, this easy disconnectedness, that grants him his curious sense of liberty . . .

IS HE SPLIT? IS HE PSYCHOTIC?!

that frees him up to saunter boldly . . .

ARROGANTLY!

and audaciously . . .

ZERO MANNERS!

into the artificial confines of 'art' and 'film' and . . .

. . . SORRY?

'culture' . . .

. . . WHAT?

to gaze at them (frankly, openly) . . .

A NUTTER!

and then to poke out his tongue at them . . .

RUDE!

(if he feels the urge) . . .

IMPULSIVE!

without any hint of sophistry or self-consciousness . . .

RIDICULOUSLY NAIVE!

Without showiness . . .

QUIET. CUNNING.

Without (at least almost without) . . .

A WILD BEAST!

Compunction . . .

SURELY *HE* OPERATES WITHOUT COMPUNCTION
BECAUSE *WE* OPERATE *WITH CONSTRAINT?*
ONE NECESSARILY PERMITS THE OTHER?
WE ARE CONSTRAINED SO *HE* IS FREE?
ARE *WE* NOT THE ONES PAYING FOR THIS?
ARE *WE* NOT THE ONES SUPPORTING THIS?
ARE *WE* NOT THE ONES ENABLING THIS?
WE!
ME!
YOU!
US!
SURELY *HE* EXISTS BECAUSE *WE* CONSTRAIN OURSELVES?
SURELY WE *CREATE* HIM?
WE *ALLOW* HIM?
HE IS *NOT* FREE!
WE *ALLOW* HIM HIS FREEDOM, AND IN SO DOING

WE *UNDERMINE OUR OWN.*
WE *MAKE* HIM FREE!
THIS IS *OUR* GIFT!
WITHOUT *US* HE IS NOTHING!
NOTHING!
HE *THINKS* HE'S FREE . . .
BUT WE OWN HIM!
HE BELONGS *TO US!*
HE IS OURS!

Concentrate, Fi.
Concentrate.
Stop being perpetually sidelined by . . .

Back to the top.

. . . and it is this . . . this quiet steadiness, this easy disconnectedness, that grants him his curious sense of liberty, that frees him up to saunter boldly and audaciously into the artificial confines of . . .

No.
No.

Fi Kinebuchi grabs her phone again. She is shaken.

Did you read the Martin O'Keefe piece about TonyInterruptor? she types.

What IS it about this whole scenario that's getting people so fired up?
The comments!
It feels like I'm playing a bit part in a blockbuster about Nikola Tesla or DB Cooper.
And now, apparently, he's a multi-millionaire art mover. He transports art, internationally . . .

Two hours later. Her phone pings.

Sorry, Fi. Mallory had a bad fall. Sprained wrist, potentially a broken ankle. All pretty chaotic here. Can you forward the link? XL

10

'I know I shouldn't really say anything because I'm actually a little bit high on painkillers right now ... um ...' Mallory screws her eyes shut behind her sunglasses and slowly shakes her head (as if by shaking her head she might miraculously alleviate the extraordinary halo of light that currently surrounds Sasha Keyes – yes, *Sasha Keyes* – as he sits beside her, in the main hospital reception area, waiting for transport, like a slightly grumpy, crumpled and bemused angel) ...

'... Um ... *yeah!* I worry that I may be a little bit high on painkillers right now ...' she repeats, opening her eyes and stabilising her sunglasses with a poorly bandaged index finger (Sasha Keyes is *still* sitting beside her, in the main hospital reception area, waiting for transport, like a slightly grumpy, crumpled and bemused angel ... although ... although some angels are *avenging* angels, aren't they? Or *dark* angels? So she supposes this must actually make some kind of surreal-tinged sense ...?).

'... I usually have a strict narcotics ...' she scowls, struggling to find the right word, '... embargo ...? I mean I was in NA for many years ... many, many years ... Like ... like a *loooong* time. A *looong, looong* time.'

Mallory inspects the ceiling for a moment while gathering her thoughts.

'NA is a *cult*. Everyone says it. We all said it. I was like ... regular as clockwork ... AA, NA ... five, sometimes six times a week ... until I got thrown out of the local chapters for plain-speaking ... for being ... um ... too frank ... too analytical? Insufficiently ... um ... kind? Empathetic? But I was just *paying attention*, Sasha. You know? I mean is anyone – is *anyone* – paying attention in the Modern Era? Aside from *moi*, obviously? Am I the *only* person paying attention in the Modern Era?'

She frowns, and before Sasha Keyes has a chance to respond ...

'The "Modern Era"?' she murmurs, slowly turning her tongue around these words and feeling them quietly calcify in her mouth – becoming all powdery and earthy and minerally; 'Urgh. Is that even ...? Is that ...?'

'Well *I'm* paying attention,' Sasha interjects, slightly irritated.

(Sasha Keyes is an improvisational musician. He is a High Priest of focus. He *never* stops paying attention. Too risky).

'Um ... is that even "a thing"?' Mallory continues (undeterred by Sasha's interjection), casually air quoting but with a semblance – just a semblance – of irony, 'I mean ...' Mallory air quotes again, '... "The Modern Era"? Or am I ... am I literally just one level above sitting here and drooling?'

She ponders this for a moment, then adds: 'Did I just say "*moi*" instead of 'me'? Have these painkillers made me both stupid *and* an arsehole?'

Sasha Keyes takes his time in responding. Initially it's because he's not sure if Mallory has finished externalising what he suspects may actually be an internal monologue. Subsequently it's because he's in two minds as to whether this is the kind of social encounter in which active participation is either wise or necessary. He suppresses a nervous yawn.

'To be perfectly honest,' he finally drawls (No wonder she's a damn lawyer! All these infernal *questions*!), '... or perfectly ... uh ... "*frank*", if you prefer ...?'

Mallory nods emphatically (Perfectly honest. Good. Perfectly frank. Yup – that'll be *just* the ticket ...).

'Well, while I can't pretend to fathom the overall impact of powerful narcotics on your intelligence, brain function, personality etc.,' he reasons, 'what I *do* know, and on fairly good authority, is that your reputation as "an unholy bitch" is celebrated through all of North Kent – possibly even beyond.' (Sasha also air quotes, but in his case it's as a devastating satire of Mallory's previous air quoting).

'Huh?' Mallory looks confused (it's not the actual content of what he's just said that disarms her, so much as the exquisite combination of terrible honesty *and* savage parody).

'Have you ever stopped to think that maybe it isn't just

the painkillers?' he expands, thoughtfully, 'That maybe it's just . . .' he shrugs, '*you*?'

Mallory processes this information for approximately three (admittedly, very long) seconds then bursts into peals of laughter. Sasha's eyes widen.

Mallory has an extraordinary laugh: loud – infectious – free.

'You're right! I *am* an Unholy Bitch!'

Mallory pumps her remaining workable fist in triumph, 'I honestly *am*!'

She beams at Sasha Keyes, '*You're* the arsehole.'

A hospital cleaner wanders past pushing a mop in the guise of a broom. Sasha appraises Mallory, balefully. He inspects his watch. He sighs deeply. It is 3.15 a.m. Will this night *never end*?

Mallory has already shifted focus and is temporarily fixating on the blue Asics trainer on her one un-bandaged foot (the other trainer is in her bag). 'Trainers are *so weird*,' she muses, 'So . . . *insubstantial* . . . like a sweet wrapper . . . No. It's more like . . . it's more like my foot has been devoured by a voracious synthetic reptile. A strange blue reptile. I don't know . . . they're so *impermanent*, Sasha . . . so *soft*.'

Mallory continues to appraise her foot with a kind of horrified fascination.

'I believe everything after the Middle Ages is generally described as "Modern",' Sasha finally takes pity on her, 'It's a fairly loose classification. Although I guess if we felt like being especially twatty then we might call ourselves "Post-Modern" . . .'

He shrugs, 'but Post-Modernism is more a "movement" than an "era" . . .'

'Oh my oh my,' Mallory has dragged her attention from her trainer and is now apprehending Sasha Keyes (somewhat unsteadily) with a renewed regard, 'You really *are* what it says on the tin, Sash . . .'

Mallory has raised a bandaged hand in the hope of exchanging a high five with him.

'Can I call you Sash, Sash?' she asks.

'No,' Sasha is categorical. He ignores Mallory's raised hand a) on principle, b) because he is squeamish about physical contact with strangers, c) because the wrist is bandaged (is a high five really sensible under these circumstances?), and d) (in light of c), because she's a hell-bitch lawyer, isn't she?

Mallory accepts Sasha's mulish non-compliance with equanimity (she is stoned, after all) and reaches forward to pick a tiny piece of lint from his shoulder.

'Lint,' she says, squinting down at it unsteadily through her dark glasses.

She repeats the word again, with apparent wonder.

'*Lint.*'

She pauses.

'Wow.'

She pauses again.

'Wow-*ow-ow-ow-ow-ow-ow-ow-ow.*'

'Anything will sound ridiculous if you repeat it often enough,' Sasha sighs (while quickly undertaking a rapid dandruff check; he happens to be wearing a beautifully tailored green velvet jacket), 'because words are, by their very nature, inherently ludicrous.'

Mallory cheerfully ignores him.

'*LINT!*' she enunciates, dramatically. A passing anaesthetist glances over, somewhat alarmed.

'And what exactly *does* it say on the tin?' Sasha demands, slightly tetchy (although this isn't especially remarkable as he is invariably tetchy).

'The tin? Oooh.' Mallory is temporarily distracted from her childlike wonder at the concept of 'lint', 'Well now, um ... let's see ... The Big Five?'

'The Big Four,' Sasha corrects her, drolly.

'Huh?'

'"Arsehole",' he shrugs.

'Ah yes, yes. Fair point,' Mallory acquiesces (not even a smidgeon of remorse), 'Okay ... Hmm. Gimmie a second ... uh ...' She lifts her glasses from her nose and surveys Sasha intently, as if the appropriate words might miraculously solidify at various points about his person, 'Um ... okay ... so, *arsehole*. That's safe. It's in the bag ...' She lowers her glasses again then holds up her thumb, 'And I think we already deduced that you are ...' she grins, 'a big old *smarty-pants* ...' she holds up her index finger alongside the thumb, '... and kind of ... sort of ... uh ... hmm ... a *connoisseur*? No ... no ... an *aesthete*,' she finally settles (her eyes resting on a large amethyst pinky ring that once belonged to Sasha's maternal grandfather; an Anglican bishop). She holds up three fingers, 'And ... uh ... let's not forget *grumpy*!' she adds, sniggering (she is focusing on the downturned corners of his mouth) . . . 'One more . . . one more . . .' She lifts her glasses again and closely scrutinises the tiny mouche or 'soul patch' underneath his lower lip . . . '*Ridiculous*?'

Five fingers.

Sasha inevitably bridles at 'ridiculous'. He is just about to emit a growl when . . .

'Not ridiculous. Sorry. No . . .' Mallory changes her mind . . . 'Not ridiculous . . . uh . . . *preposterous!*'

For some reason 'preposterous' (which is surely just 'ridiculous' with hidden shoe lifts) feels harder for Sasha to take umbrage at. Why though? He isn't sure.

'Thank you for this entirely balanced and measured assessment of my character,' he says.

'No problem,' Mallory releases her glasses again, '*Sarcastic*.'

Six fingers.

'Big *six* . . .' Sasha mutters.

'*Pedantic*.' Mallory adds a seventh finger.

Sasha really wants to say 'Big *seven*,' but his pride declares war on his pettiness and, miraculously, it triumphs.

A cab arrives for the woman and child sitting two chairs along from Mallory.

'The point I'm making,' Mallory continues, completely oblivious to Sasha's bridling, 'is that you can't honestly expect me to just sit here and quietly – *passively* – bear witness to your endless bullshit, your patent hypocrisy, your cowardice, your spinelessness, your profound *moral turpitude* and simply . . . *urgh* . . .' she grimaces, 'you know . . . "make space" . . .'

'Sorry?'

It takes a moment for Sasha to realise that Mallory has now moved on from her enunciation of his Big Seven and has jumped straight back into her NA-related diatribe.

'I just can't pussy-foot, Sash,' she grumbles, 'I've *never* pussy-footed. It just isn't in my nature to pussy-foot. I actually . . . I never really had the . . . you know . . . growing up . . . never really had the opportunity . . . the . . . the luxury? My priority was simply to work out what I needed; you know, the basics – food, warmth, shoes – and then, just as soon as I was physically able, to ask for them. To demand them from whosoever was there and whosoever the fuck would listen. Self-advocating. Soon as I could talk. Maybe even sooner.'

For some reason Sasha Keyes finds himself deeply moved at the idea of the tiny child Mallory asking for shoes.

Shoes.

Sasha Keyes has never had to ask for shoes. Sasha Keyes has always been automatically provided with (or has provided himself with) shoes.

'Some people never learn to ask for what they want,' Mallory shrugs, 'or to say what they really think. To . . .' she faux-gags, '. . . "speak their truth". Perhaps they never actually need to? Well, I needed to, Sash. I really needed to. It sounds a bit dramatic, but fuck it. Pussy-footing is a privilege.'

'Pussy-foot,' Sasha echoes, plainly disarmed (and disconcerted) by Mallory's cheerful show of vulnerability, 'Is that a verb?'

'We have this in common,' Mallory continues, 'You and I.

I think we have this in common, Sash. It never occurred to me until this exact moment – this precise moment. So it's . . . it's kind of like a . . . *Ka-boom!*' Mallory describes a dramatic nuclear mushroom cloud of revelation, of sudden insight, with both hands (she even includes a pitter-patter, a tinkling, of post-strike radiation).

'Sorry?' Sasha scowls, not quite following, 'You're suggesting that we're . . . um . . . kindred spirits?'

Mallory scowls back at Sasha for a second, in silence, and then: 'HELLO? *HELLO?!*' she blasts, waving her hand in front of his face like he's a smeared window that requires buffing, 'ARE YOU *PAYING ATTENTION* SASHA?!'

Sasha winces (he has hyper-sensitive hearing).

'I'm talking about PUSSY-FOOTING,' Mallory bawls, 'I'm saying that you and I – that *we* – don't pussy-foot! Neither of us. And the AWFUL TRUTH about the fucking world is that it's *ALL ABOUT* pussy-footing!' She points, indiscriminately, at various people dotted around the foyer, 'These people, these idiots, Sash, ALL of them: fucking pussy-footers!'

Sasha wonders how many times Mallory Shore can say the word pussy-foot without him completely losing his reason. He also worries that Mallory (stoned Mallory) is so invested in the painful memories of her NA rejection/battle/disappointments that she might easily forget that this has *nothing whatsoever to do with him*. He glances around, furtively. Is it possible that people close by (or further away – Mallory is quite loud) may think that she is actually exasperated with *him* (berating *him*), Sasha Keyes, when in actual fact he has good reason to be cross with *her* (given that her daughter is partially responsible for putting both his reputation and his career in jeopardy . . . um . . . online)?

So far as he is aware, Mallory Shore has yet to apologise for this minor detail. In fact Mallory Shore seems to have *no intention whatsoever* of apologising for this minor detail.

'Pussy foot!' Mallory chuckles (her mood suddenly switching from one of rampant exasperation to one of childish delight). 'Like a little, teeny-tiny pussy foot! Pussy foots. Four foots. Four pussy foots.'

Although she *is* stoned, Sasha rationalises, and . . . yes . . . quite beautiful. A kind of uncompromising . . . a stark beauty. Dignified. Thin. Like a slivered almond. No. There's more gravitas to it – to her beauty – than that. It's less whimsical. She's like . . . she's like . . . hard to articulate . . . an incredibly well-carved gravestone?

He glances at her, sideways . . . She's also . . . in contrast to the vast proportion of gravestones . . . she's actually quite entertaining. Not 'funny' so much as . . . as . . . *comical.* Is this intentional? Is this her personality – her essential nature? Or is it narcotically induced? Hmm. He has no evidence that a stoned person is intrinsically more entertaining than a non-stoned person. They're possibly just . . . just looser. A looser version of themselves. Less constrained by convention, but still, fundamentally, the same person.

The sad fact is that Sasha doesn't generally find too much in the world to be amused by. He has high standards and he prides himself on them. He's a perfectionist. He has to be, doesn't he? Because practice makes perfect?

Sasha Keyes brings his perfectionism to all areas of his life; especially to improvising (he holds his perfectionism on his lap, leans forward and cocoons it with his body and forearms, growling protectively, like it's a newly hatched yellow chick).

Sasha Keyes must improvise *flawlessly*; to the highest possible standard. I mean where's the point in doing *anything* without finesse? Without confidence? Without complete self-assurance? To know your subject inside out . . . to show mastery . . . to be . . . to be exemplary. It all takes concentration. It takes *work*. Naturally it requires talent, too, and opportunity . . . connection . . . passion . . . But fundamentally it demands focus. Self-control. Restraint. Persistence. Fortitude. Sacrifice.

And practice.

Yes . . . practice. Life is not a dress rehearsal. But for Sasha Keyes, life *is* a dress rehearsal.

There's a whole lot of rehearsing.

Ah. Now surely *that's* one of my Big Five, he muses: *Serious?*

'Perhaps I'm just too serious,' he murmurs, half to himself.

Too serious?

Doesn't *someone* have to take things seriously, though? Does the ENTIRE FUCKING WORLD need to spend all its spare time idly watching cat videos on TikTok?

Is taking things seriously a criminal offence now?

'*Lighten up*, kiddo!'

Remember? His artist dad? Rolling home from his studio at

all hours? Overalled, paint-splattered, reeking of turps, fags and booze?
Charismatic? Exuberant? Sarcastic? Always finding new ways to belittle tiny, bespectacled, deathly serious Sasha in front of his piano teacher mum? And how his mum (who hardly ever stopped playing the straight guy, the practical one, the sensible one, who hardly ever stopped worrying about the deadlines and the bills and the packing of school lunches) . . . how this woman (one minute so weighed down, so attentive, so reliable) was suddenly transformed – enlivened, *seduced* – by his father's easy charm into laughing along?

Sasha never found the joke funny.

What was the joke?

Was *he* the joke?

Little Sasha? So morose? So dutiful? So eager to demonstrate his solidity, his consistency, his devotion?

When precisely was the last time that he (adult Sasha, fully grown Sasha) really laughed at something (not sarcastically)? A full belly laugh?

Oh. Um. Has he *ever* experienced a full belly laugh?

Sasha thinks hard. *The King of Comedy*. He'd watched a special screening a couple of weeks back at the Gulbenkian. Hadn't seen it in years. It had made him laugh. But a full belly laugh? Or a peal? A peal of laughter? Like Mallory's earlier proper-church-bell peal?

Should I laugh more? he wonders. Isn't it my duty as an adept – a genius – improviser? Because surely laughter's always improvised? A random act? Spontaneous? Unplanned?

In the way that a vast proportion of the truly great things in life are unplanned and spontaneous? These things are, by their very nature, responsive . . . reactive. No. *Inter*active. *Communal.* An exchange. A free exchange. Truly felt. In the belly. The gut.

He scowls. Oh God. Perhaps laughter is actually the final frontier? One of the last remaining *authentically* spontaneous acts?

Hang on. He freezes. Am I unwittingly straying into Kinebuchi territory, here? The idea of laughter as a truly *radical* act? Isn't this precisely why the Buddha is so often depicted (in sculptures and in artworks) as smiling and laughing? Because the Buddha has no time for 'form' (for rules) or for ego (passion, greed, ambition, anger), and the best (or gentlest) way of breaking the spell of these things is simply to laugh at them?

Hmm. He blinks. Does that render laughing more radical *even* than improvised jazz? He scratches his chin, unsmiling. (Surely no interior monologue about laughter has ever been conceptualised quite so gravely, so humourlessly . . .?)

Sasha Keyes inspects the light fittings as he ruminates. His eye is held briefly by what seems to be netting which (he presumes) is there to prevent pigeons from perching.

But laughter . . . yes . . . laughter is automatic . . . unthinking . . . effortless . . . Even cruel laughter (like his dad's) . . . whereas improvised jazz is both completely spontaneous *and* deeply considered . . . also effort-full. It's hard work.

Should it be, though? Should it be effortful? Surely all the tedious rehearsal is a way of creating a safety net (a net of skill, a net of muscle memory) so that during performance the spirit is free to just . . . to just fly . . . to just sing, *without* effort?

Is that what TonyInterruptor was implying? About honesty?

Sasha Keyes grimaces.

'I mean to just do nothing. To bite my tongue . . .' (Mallory is still talking), 'To *say* nothing. Because man, this is *hardcore.* You know? I have *no time* to fuck around, Sash. Life is short. Things to do. I have a child with special needs . . .'

(Oh. Okay. She has a child with special needs. Sasha straightens his spine a little – although a description of his posture has yet to be published in the British media without the liberal application of the adverb 'ramrod'.)

'. . . Noses and bums to wipe,' Mallory grumbles, 'Hair to oil. Places to go. Appointments to keep. There you have it. My sodding life. My whole mundane life. In a little walnut shell. Like a beautifully carved walnut shell. No. Even smaller. Like a hazelnut shell. Very small. A very small life. A very small shell. A little shell. Carved into the shape of a hermit crab. Or maybe a perfect, curled-up dormouse . . . a thing of . . . you know . . . fragile . . . of delicate beauty . . . so long as you aren't afraid of mice. Or allergic to walnuts.'

'Hazelnuts,' Sasha corrects her (he is allergic to pecans).

(Um . . . Hair to oil?!)

*

'*Punctilious!*' Mallory exclaims, delighted, looking up from her cupped palm. The palm has been cupped to gently contain the world's most perfect dormouse *netsuke*. She relinquishes the imaginary dormouse *netsuke* and raises eight solemn fingers.

Sasha Keyes stares at Mallory Shore, somewhat perplexed and almost . . . well . . . (he struggles to admit this) . . . almost *intrigued*. Mallory Shore is extremely troublesome, very high on ketamine (do they *seriously* give people with broken limbs ketamine nowadays?) and horribly difficult to corral. Wholesomely unwholesome. Confusingly precise and sharp – even circumspect – yet still kind of . . . of wild and unfiltered. To all intents and purposes Mallory Shore *is* improvised jazz! His favourite thing in all the world. His life's chosen conduit for meaning. His first and final reference point. His *being*.

Like improvised jazz Mallory Shore is impossible to wrangle! Maddeningly spontaneous! Beautiful. Crazy. Powerful. Chaotic. *True*. At its – and, perhaps, her – best: completely devastating. Devastatingly lovely. Devastatingly fragile.

'Aren't pedantic and punctilious basically interchangeable?' Sasha wonders.

'Hmm.' Mallory ponders. She chews on her lower lip, thinking deeply, then: 'Let's just upgrade them both to "meticulous".'

Meticulous?

'Okay.'

Sasha Keyes smiles. He likes meticulous.

Mallory Shore observes Sasha Keyes smiling and struggles to read her own complicated emotional response to it.

What *is* this feeling?

Congruence? Rapport? Harmony?

Possibly something musical. Fleeting. Like the first few notes of a song . . .

Another question: Is Sasha Keyes developing a little *crush* on Mallory Shore (wrong-footed and sprained-wristed Kentish married mother of two)? Because love (like laughter, and like improvised jazz) is also utterly unpredictable, impossible to wrangle . . . maddeningly spontaneous. Beautiful. Crazy. Powerful. Chaotic. *True.*

And serendipitous.

'Serendipitous!' he muses. He is no longer smiling. He is lost in thought again. Surely so much of what is improvised in jazz depends on coincidence? An unexpected coming-together? A brief communion? Kismet?

'How the hell did we both end up here?' he wonders, glancing over towards the beautiful tombstone that is Mallory Shore, feeling borderline outraged. He is suddenly torn between the idea that the world makes *no* sense and the opposing notion that the world makes *perfect* sense. Might it even be both?

Woah.

Mallory is holding her iPhone and trying, unsuccessfully, to open it with facial recognition technology.

'My face isn't working, Sash,' she murmurs, 'My face has stopped working. I expect it's the pain . . . It must be the pain . . . or maybe it's the drugs.'

'Pain can be transformative,' Sasha concurs, leaning over to inspect her phone, 'but I suspect you're just low on battery.'

'I *am*,' Mallory sighs. 'I'm so fucking low on battery, Sash. I am spent. I am *done*. Fucking *done*. Thank you for noticing that. Thank you for seeing that.'

Mallory Shore reaches out her bandaged hand and places it onto Sasha Keyes's leg. She silently articulates her profound sense of gratitude at his clear apprehension of her scandalously low levels of battery by dint of a small squeeze.

(For the record, Sasha Keyes is not – and has never been – someone whose leg might be gratefully squeezed. There is an invisible force field that generally precludes it, which is informally called his 'fundamental essence').

Sasha Keyes stares, astonished, at Mallory Shore's hand on his leg.

'Ow,' Mallory says (her wrist hurts). She removes her hand.

How the hell did they both end up here?

Here.

'How the hell did we both end up here, Mallory?' he asks. No bells or whistles.

(Although a little bell does ring way up in the heavenly spheres, because this is the first time *ever* that Sasha Keyes has used Mallory Shore's name. Those three sacred syllables! They are bouncing around his mouth, playing ping-pong with his tongue, his breath.)

*

How?

Mallory turns to gaze at him, owlishly, her chin lowered, as if she has an invisible pair of pince-nez perched on her nose.

Is this . . .? Are they possibly having . . . 'a moment'?

Okay.

How precisely *did* they end up here?

So far as he (Sasha Keyes) can recollect, Mallory (her general intention/motive/purpose unknown) had whizzed past him on her clanking wheelchair as he sat muttering to himself, impatiently, in the hospital reception area. He was waiting for his ride home. She had sworn (loudly), ground to a sudden halt, twirled around, reversed, shoved another chair aside with her bandaged foot and then planted herself next to him.

'Shhhh!' she stage-whispered (finger to her lips), then silently mouthed, 'INCOGNITO!'

She fished around in her bag (slung jauntily over the back of her wheelchair), pulled out a pair of sunglasses and put them on.

Her handling of the wheelchair is so proficient that Sasha can't help but think that she has used one for much of her adult life. He has no real way of knowing, though, and it would be impertinent to ask.

Mallory Shore is also (it seems – but he isn't entirely sure) waiting for a cab. Several nurses have walked past and gazed at her with something amounting to concern. He doesn't really understand why this is.

Why might this be?

She appears to have broken her arm and sprained her ankle. Perhaps she's cracked a bone in her foot? There may also be the early stages of a black eye.

'I know who you are,' Mallory Shore whispers, 'but you do not know who *I* am . . .' she glances, anxiously, over her shoulder (although she is parked against a wall), 'My name is Mallory Shore. I am the adoptive mother of India Shore. I arrived here in an ambulance. Um. I arrived here in the back of an ambulance,' she modifies, 'I was not driving the ambulance. They gave me ketamine. And I know I shouldn't really say anything as I *am* a little bit high on painkillers right now . . .'

Mallory Shore is inspecting Sasha Keyes in the present moment, somewhat disappointed, 'You claimed to be paying attention, Sasha,' she announces, 'I hate to say it, but there was almost a . . . a tinge of . . . um . . . *arrogance* in your demeanour . . .'

'I *did* claim to be paying attention,' Sasha nods, 'And I *was* paying attention. I am.'

'Tinge,' Mallory repeats, then snorts: 'Tin-*n*-*n*-*n*-ge.'

'Yup.'

Sasha acknowledges the universal truth that 'tinge' is an entertaining word.

'I arrived in the back of an ambulance,' Mallory reiterates, 'Didn't I say that? Earlier?'

'You did,' Sasha confirms, 'and I applaud you for being so

literal. Although the question, when I asked it, was more . . . more metaphysical . . . philosophical. As in: "How did *we* end up here?" . . . You and I. Together. It feels . . . unlikely. It feels a little far-fetched and almost . . . well, serendipitous.'

'Right?! What are the chances?!' Mallory exclaims, 'One moment I'm watching you denigrate Fi Kinebuchi online and receiving veiled threats from your manager, the next . . .'

'This isn't even my local A&E,' Sasha continues, 'I live on the outskirts of Maidstone. I'd popped into IKEA to get a kind of . . . a plant stand . . . for my aspidistra, and they didn't have it in stock . . . which was extremely annoying . . .' Mallory yawns.

'Very boring, I know,' he concedes.

'Just . . . yeah . . . interminable,' Mallory concurs.

'I see now why you got thrown out of AA,' Sasha notes.

'I quit!' Mallory giggles.

'Anyway. And then this *indigestion* which had been plaguing me all day just . . . it suddenly . . . WHAM! It explodes inside my chest. Like a kind of . . . a jackhammer. The paramedic on the ambulance thought it was a panic attack . . . but I wasn't *feeling* especially panicked . . .' Sasha shrugs, 'so they brought me in. As a precaution. Although it was possibly just a ploy to distract me from . . .'

'Who?' Mallory interrupts, 'Who was trying to distract you . . .?'

'The paramedic.'

'Which paramedic?' Mallory demands.

'Perhaps it was just an attempt to keep me calm?'
Sasha Keyes sighs. He checks his phone. No messages. From anyone.

'I was just . . . literally . . . I was sitting at my desk,' Mallory nods, 'and I was gazing at my laptop. Boring legal documents. You know, pretending to work. And then I suddenly started fantasising about Daniel Andersen Lie . . .'

'Who?' Sasha glances up from his phone.

'Daniel Andersen Lie.'

Mallory frowns.

'Hang on. No. Anders Danielsen Lie.'

'Anders Danielsen Lie?'

Sasha is none the wiser.

Mallory's head flips around. Her head moves so quickly that her glasses lift then land, slightly askew, on her nose.

'You don't know who Anders Danielsen Lie is?'

She neglects to adjust them.

'I do not. *Should* I know who Anders Danielsen Lie is?'

Sasha Keyes doesn't seem especially concerned by his insufficient awareness of the living/breathing life of Anders Danielsen Lie (although he *is* somewhat irritated by Mallory's wonky glasses).

'*Fuck yes.*' Mallory is appalled. 'You *really* should know. I mean . . . *Re*-prise?!'

She dabs at her lip with her sleeve. 'Oooh. I'm . . . My lip suddenly feels all . . . um . . . baggy . . .'

Sasha pats around inside his pocket for a handkerchief and finds one. He offers it to her.

'Aw. Thanks.' Mallory takes it. The handkerchief is clean and decorated with musical notes.

'That's so cute!' she squeaks, 'Aw! Musical notes! So cute. And also . . . kind of . . . I dunno . . .' she starts to frown, 'unbearably corny. Um . . . what's that word? Reductive? Is that the word? Reductive?'

Mallory pats at her lip with the handkerchief. She still doesn't straighten her glasses.

'I get sent this stuff,' Sasha shrugs, 'It's promotional.'

'I mean for someone whose entire *oeuvre* is . . . is experimental, is improvised, is . . . God, yes. You *should* know about Anders Danielsen Lie,' Mallory shakes her head, appalled. The glasses re-settle on her nose, much to Sasha's relief. 'Fuck yes. You should *certainly* know who Daniel is . . . um . . . I mean . . . Fuck. That depresses me. That Sasha Kaye, of all people, doesn't know who . . .'

'Keyes,' Sasha interrupts.

'Uh-huh. Him. Musical keys. Hand-key-chief.'
She pauses, 'Is Kaye his *real* name?'

'*Keyes*. Keyes is *my* real name. Yes.'
Silence.

'I get asked that a lot.'

'Of course you do!' Mallory nods, wisely, 'Of course you get asked that a lot! It's a very sensible question to ask a person. Of course you get asked that!'
Silence.

'My dad was a successful painter – a famous abstract artist. I hated him. When I began to play music professionally I decided to use my mother's name. She was called Marian Keyes. She was a piano teacher. And a piano tuner.'

'What's your preferred key?' Mallory wonders, 'A, B or C?' Sasha sighs, 'Do you even know what a key *is*, Mallory Shore?'

'Of course I do!' Mallory is scandalised, 'Of course I know what a key is. And please stop addressing me like an irritated Victorian schoolmaster.'

If truth be told, Mallory Shore actually *likes* the way Sasha Keyes uses her whole name. When Sasha Keyes says her whole name she likes the sound of who she is – of who she might be. And that's very strange, because she *doesn't* actually like who she is. She *doesn't* actually like Mallory Shore. Not at all. How maddening.

She absolutely hates herself.

'Excuse me? Hello? Everyone?' Sasha is pretending to address the assembled pussy-footers (none of whom are actively listening, although most of whom are idly listening): 'Mallory Shore doesn't appear to have the *slightest* idea of what a key is.' (Sasha wonders what it feels like to listen idly. He doesn't really know what that would feel like because he listens so actively. Active listening is his joy and his responsibility – possibly even his curse.)

'What were we talking about?' Mallory demands (unmoved by Sasha's pitiable attempt to humiliate her, publicly), 'Before? I feel like it was important. But I'm high on . . .'

'Painkillers.' Sasha nods.

'Danielsen . . . um . . . Anders . . .' he reminds her, after a few seconds.

'Anders Danielsen ... Yes!' Mallory's spirits are immediately revived, 'You should google! Go on. Google him. You know ...' she lifts her glasses and gazes into Sasha face, scrutinising him intently, her pupils so huge that they seem to take up 75% of the space in her eyes.

'You *are* handsome,' she observes, 'but it's really hard to see it at first because of your awful personality.'

'Thank you.' Sasha nods.

'*Awful*,' she reiterates, 'And just look at you, Sash: a modern man in green velvet. Stuffy but with a side order of grandiosity. And the ring!' she cackles, 'The pinky ring!'

'If words were bullets I'd be riddled with gunshot right now,' Sasha muses, 'I'd be terminally wounded. But thank you.'

He smiles.

'Honest, though?' Mallory continues, patently on a roll, 'Is Sasha *honest*? Everyone?' (again, the pussy-footers are called to witness), 'Fuck yes! Absolutely! Sasha is a straight dealer. None more so. None. Sasha Keyes is one hundred percent sincere.'

'Oh, Okay.'

(Sasha wonders if Mallory Shore might've forgotten, once again, that *he* is, in fact, Sasha Keyes.)

'I was thinking about this earlier,' Mallory continues, 'and it's possible that what I'm about to say is kind of ... I don't know ... borderline-offensive, but ...'

'Then maybe ...' Sasha holds up his flattened palm (This is British Sign Language for STOP).

'. . . but I'm gonna say it anyway,' Mallory shrugs, 'I'm just gonna say it . . .'

'Don't say it,' Sasha counsels.

'I must say it. I have to say it. It's like a compulsion. I must say it.'

'Well . . .' Sasha closes his eyes in order to compose himself, 'Fine.'

'Okay. So the upshot of what I was thinking earlier – and I'm still thinking it – is that he wouldn't have dared open his mouth . . . that li'l rat . . . TonyInterruptor. I mean . . . he would *never* have dared say you weren't honest . . . questioned your integrity, musical or otherwise . . . he couldn't have said *any* of it if you weren't white. If you were black. It's simply your *whiteness* that makes you vulnerable to attack here.'

Sasha peeks through slitted eyelids at Mallory Shore.

'I don't really know how to respond to that,' he says (honestly).

'It was a CHEAP SHOT, Sash, just a CHEAP SHOT! He was bullying *you*. The little twat. *He's* the bully.'

'I hear what you're saying,' Sasha tries to be gentle, 'and I appreciate the vote of confidence . . . the . . . you know . . . support. But I just don't think it's an especially helpful . . . I mean if what we are doing here is skirting around concepts like soulfulness . . . what is soulful. What "the blues" are. Legacy. Authenticity. History . . .'

'I'm not "skirting",' Mallory announces, 'I don't "skirt". "Skirting" is pussy-footing by any other name and I don't pussy-foot.'

'Oh God,' Sasha murmurs, 'Not . . .'

Pussy-foot.

'In the world of jazz,' Mallory interrupts, 'you will always be a second-class citizen. Doesn't matter how hard you try or how talented you are. You will always be open to gentle ridicule. And that's . . .' Mallory shakes her head, 'That's FUCKING SAD.'

Sasha stares at her, frowning. 'But is it really *that* sad?' he counters, 'As things go? Is it really *that* unjust? I mean, I have the choice to love any musical genre and I choose to love – or am drawn to – a genre which is traditionally, predominantly black . . . but it's precisely this legacy which makes it feel . . .'

'For the record, I am of mixed race,' Mallory interrupts, 'so I don't need to skirt or to pussy-foot. I can just say what the hell I like.'

'I am not contesting that point,' Sasha holds up both hands in a gesture of compliance, 'That point has been fully . . .'

'I suppose it all just boils down to how truly free it is actually, conceivably possible to be. In life. In art. Even in free jazz. We live . . . no, we *subsist* inside these tight little coffins of form, of convention . . .'

'Hmm, a small side-serving of Kinebuchi-style relativism,' Sasha observes, wearily.

'I have a very dark heart, Sash,' Mallory confesses.

'You do?'

'Pickled,' Mallory nods, 'in formaldehyde.'

'Hmm. I wonder how that feels?' Sasha muses.

'Like absolute crap,' Mallory confides.

Sasha momentarily interrogates his own heart. His own heart feels a tiny bit spongy and loose by comparison to Mallory Shore's dark heart. He likes the comparison. He likes how Mallory Shore makes him feel. She makes him feel . . . lighter.

'IT'S NOT FAIR, Sash!' Mallory is suddenly caught up in the emotion of her argument again, '*Why* is the world so unbelievably ARSE-FACED? *Why?!*'

'Well, I suppose in the great scheme of things . . .' Sasha shrugs, resigned.

He's enjoying playing the reasonable part, for once. He *likes* being reasonable. It feels . . . it feels bigger. Expansive.

'Huh?' Mallory turns and gazes at Sasha Keyes (as if she hasn't even the slightest idea who he is), then her head snaps back again as two nurses materialise directly in front of her, one of whom is burly and male.

'Oh! Hello,' Sasha says, slightly disconcerted.

'Mallory?' The male nurse addresses Mallory calmly but firmly, 'Mrs Shore? We're going to need to ask you to accompany us back to the treatment room.'

'*Taxi for Sasha Keyes!*' a voice calls through the foyer.

'Just one second,' Mallory tells the nurses. 'I need to tell Sasha Keyes something important. This is Sasha Keyes.' Mallory introduces Sasha Keyes to the nurses.

'Hello.' Sasha stands and starts to button up his green velvet jacket.

'You're really going to want to hear this, Sasha,' Mallory persists, 'it'll set everything into perspective.'

'*Taxi for Sasha Keyes!*' the driver calls again.

Sasha raises his arm, in acknowledgement of the driver's call, but stays put.

'Okay,' he says, 'Hit me.'

'*Lionel Asbo*,' Mallory hits him.

'Sorry?' Sasha frowns.

'*Lionel Asbo*,' Mallory repeats, 'Remember? The novel? By Martin Amis? Got a mixed reception in . . . um . . . can't remember . . .?'

'What?' Sasha frowns.

'You didn't come up with the phrase, Sasha!' Mallory is triumphant, 'TonyInterruptor. It isn't yours. And it isn't Mark E Smith's, either. It's Martin's. Can't you hear it? Lionel Asbo? TonyInterruptor? The rhythm? The symmetry? The implicit snideness? You simply *improvised* on Martin's original. You adapted *his* phrase. You unconsciously adapted *Martin*'s phrase.'

'Um . . .' Sasha is processing. He continues to frown.

'And who knows, maybe Martin was originally channelling a Fall song? Maybe Mark E Smith was hidden away in there somewhere? It seems improbable . . . but who cares? The important thing is that it *isn't yours*,' Mallory repeats, 'It was already floating around in the ether like so much cultural flotsam. It belongs to the collective unconscious. It's *ours*.'

'Oh.' Sasha is momentarily flummoxed. But he is also, unexpectedly, oddly relieved.

'This whole thing,' Mallory continues, 'is just a comedy of errors, Sash. It's just much ado about . . .'

'I'm sorry to interrupt, Mrs Shore,' the female nurse interrupts, 'but the anaesthetic . . .'

'A series of mis-steps,' Sasha concurs.

'Mis-steps?' Mallory echoes.

'Yeah. It's a Buddhist idea: the Lineage of Mis-steps. In this particular tradition it's not the things we get *right* which somehow, miraculously, lead to enlightenment, but the things we get *wrong*. Fucking up is the whole ... uh ... Are you okay Mallory?'

There is a haunted expression on Mallory's face.

'*Taxi for Sasha Keyes!*'

The nurses are already turning her chair.

'Hang on ... hang on ... You're saying that even dickheads like you and me – like us – can attain ... you know ... enlightenment?' Mallory's eyes are full of tears, 'Just by ... by persistently but sincerely falling arse-over-tit?'

'The Lineage of Mis-steps,' Sasha repeats, then glances nervously over his shoulder (almost as if expecting to see a smug Fi Kinebuchi standing there).

'Serendip ... seren ...' Mallory murmurs, 'You were right, Sash. This is important. I really feel it, right here, in my ...' Mallory clutches at her stomach, her gut. Then 'Ow!' (she's used her injured hand).

'It's hard being soft,' the male nurse grins.

'Oh God ...' Mallory's eyes fill with tears, 'It's *so fucking hard* being soft.'

Sasha sighs. Yes. It *is* hard being soft, he thinks. It's actually exhausting. *Fuck* vulnerability.

'Sash?' Mallory lunges for his arm (and misses), 'Could you take a note for me, Sash? About this? You know? The Lineage of Mis-steps? In case I forget? And this other thing.

This hard being soft thing? I really need to hear it when I'm sober. Could you do that for me, Sash? Take a note?'

'I'll take a note,' Sasha assures her.

'I'm deadly serious, Sash!' Mallory is deadly serious. 'This is a *real* conversation. I'm being deadly serious.'

She turns to the nurses, '*Is* this a real conversation? Or is Sasha Keyes an angel?'

'Are you Sasha Keyes?' the male nurse asks.

'Well I'm no angel,' Sasha Keyes confirms.

'He's real,' the female nurse informs Mallory.

'Are *you* real?' Mallory asks the female nurse. They are wheeling her away.

'Hey! Hey!' Mallory turns and yells, 'I've got your hanky, Sash! I'm keeping your hanky!'

She waves the hanky in the air like a flag, 'As evidence!' she yells. But then, as she disappears through two swing doors, she squeals:

'SAVE ME SASHA! PLEEEEAAAASE!'

Sasha frowns. He is torn. He nervously hums something under his breath. A part of him wants – no, not wants, *longs* – to save Mallory Shore. But that would represent a big responsibility, surely? A huge responsibility? To save Mallory Shore? Sasha Keyes is 98% committed to a life in improvised jazz. The remaining 2% curses as it empties out the grounds from his cafetière and dutifully pays his Home Insurance bills. Sasha Keyes is 98% committed to HIS ART, and it is this part – this 98% committed part – that just wants to clamber into his waiting taxi. Go home. *Rest.*

He hums again.

Okay. He bites his lip and starts to move, tapping his inside jacket pocket, distractedly, hoping he might find the comforting nub of an HB pencil hidden away there.

SECOND PART:

INTUITIVE CONSTRUCTIONS

1

'*Ici* . . . *Juste* . . . uh . . . Right here. *Voi?* Can you . . . uh . . .?'
The gallery Registrar bounces gently from be-trainered foot to be-trainered foot in front of the artwork, 'It's just . . . uh . . . just *très problème* with *le légère* . . . *non* . . . uh trip . . . *trip* . . . uh . . . *mécanisme de déclenchement* . . .'
She stops bouncing, somewhat short of breath now, and turns to look, enquiringly, at the Art Handler.

'Trip Mechanism?' she reiterates, in perfect English.
There is a clear suggestion of deference, even a slight awkwardness, in her manner.

John Lincoln Braithwaite is frowning. He is gazing down at an iPad.

'Uh . . . *nous allons* . . . uh . . . *le besoin* Marvin,' he scowls, 'I helped install this show at the *Biennale*. I hate to *le stress* . . . *stresser* you out, but the director almost suffered an embolism.'

'*Argh.* Tell me something I *don't* know,' the Registrar groans, 'I absolutely *adore* the work when I caught it at JD Malat in London, but I . . . uh . . . was feeling then – and at some level I am *still* feeling . . . *se sentir* – that the *technologie* . . . is somewhat . . . uh . . . "surfeit to requirements" . . .'
John Lincoln Braithwaite ponders this idea, then shrugs.

'It's been said,' he offers, flatly: '*Parait-il* . . .'

The Registrar nods. She doesn't appear to be offended by this somewhat gnomic response.

'Emilien – the gallery owner – is obsessed,' she sighs, 'Completely *obsédé*. He own two pieces and has already schedule the artists' latest show for early next year.'

'Uh-huh. *Termite*,' John Lincoln Braithwaite nods, his expression unreadable.

'Yes! *Ah oui*.' The Registrar faux-shudders, grinning.
John Lincoln Braithwaite inspects the Registrar from the corner of his eye as she, in turn, quietly studies the beautifully lit, touchingly intimate film of a woman deftly arranging her hair which is being projected, as they talk, onto a large white cube. The Registrar's name is Hawi. It says as much on her lanyard. John Lincoln Braithwaite is (in spite of himself) fascinated by her skin, which is a bluey-black in hue. It's incredibly dark. On the two brief occasions that John Lincoln Braithwaite has met her previously she has been wearing white. He suspects that she only ever wears white (she is a gallery Registrar, after all). The sole exception to this rule are her large, square, thick-framed glasses, which are a matt black. Her skin shines, darkly luminous, behind

them. The Registrar is small and plump and of indeterminate age (31? 38?). Her hair is short and neatly braided into thick cornrows.

'Shore is an architect,' John Lincoln Braithwaite finally volunteers (perhaps relenting slightly), 'and Kinebuchi is a musician, so it makes perfect sense that their individual creative disciplines should find *concorde* . . . find harmony . . . around the idea of 'intuitive constructions'. All good art is about building things intuitively, be that a life, a museum, a city, a story, a song . . .'

'*Une termitière* . . .?' Hawi volunteers.

'A termite mound,' he nods, 'Exactly. The perfect example of an intuitive construction.'

'Well thank God for these, huh?' the Registrar laughs, tapping her white-trainered toe onto the polished concrete, 'Our gallery is . . . *sans danger* . . . is . . . uh . . . safe? From infestation? From *destruction*?'

'*Oui*. I imagine there will be some fairly specific requirements around lighting and temperature,' John Lincoln Braithwaite assesses the space, somewhat humourlessly, 'The gallery will need to be kept dark and cool. But from what I hear the living termites are just a small element of the whole. I think it's a wider piece about intellectual property theft, *identité, authenticity* and the nature of ideas.'

'Ah,' Hawi nods.

'Are you familiar with the writings of Eugene Marais? *The Soul of the White Ant*?'

'Uh, *non* . . .' she shakes her head, 'Although my sister,

Angweng . . . her name translate as: birthed during the season of the white ants.'

'Oh. Okay.'

John Lincoln Braithwaite turns. The film stops playing.

'*Termite*,' Hawi reiterates, 'Anweng is born in the season when the white ant moves, builds and destroys.'

'Ha. *Étrange*,' he mutters, 'Uh . . . well . . . I think *I* triggered it that time.'

He inspects the iPad.

'*Pardon?*'

'*Le film*. My movement triggered it that time.'

'*Oui*. I know. But when *I* move . . . for some reason . . . *rien* . . .' she shrugs.

'Hmm. That *is* odd. Let's swap sides.'

They swap sides.

The Registrar waits quietly as John Lincoln Braithwaite fiddles on the iPad again. After ten seconds the film starts to play from the beginning.

'Okay . . . so let's . . . uh . . .' Hawi waves her hand. The film continues to play.

'Maybe I am the ghost in the machine?' Hawi smiles, exasperated.

'The fly in the ointment,' John Lincoln Braithwaite confirms.

'The ants in our . . . uh . . .'

Hawi shimmies, mischievously. The film continues playing.

'Oh . . .' she frowns, 'Uh-oh . . .'

'*La culotte*,' John Lincoln Braithwaite completes her sentence.

They both stand and watch the film for a moment.

'It's such an ... an ... *ingénieux* ... a clever idea,' Hawi concedes, 'but as soon as the technology becomes ... uh ... unreliable, it just feels incredibly ... *agaçant* ... irritating, huh?'

'Well it's two-tiered,' John Paul Braithwaite explains, still inspecting the iPad, 'We are asked to guide our responses to what we see in two ways ... the first concerns our relationship to the artwork from the perspective of an individual – a "self" – an individual body. We need to remain still to watch the piece unfolding. If we move, if we shift, if we lift up our phone to take a picture, the film freezes and dissolves. Then the *second* tier ...'

'*Exactement*,' Hawi interrupts, 'We are obliged to be respectful because this ... this thing we watch is an intimate act. We have to gift our ... uh ... *l'immobilité* ... our stillness to the performance. In payment. In respect. *En hommage*.'

'*Precisement*,' John Lincoln Braithwaite nods, 'But then if someone else approaches, if they join you or perhaps they were there when you arrived, so if you interrupt *them* and the film stops playing ... *uh* ... then you are compromising *their* intimacy ... *their* exchange with the work ... This is your responsibility. This is your decision. It's weighted.'

'*Oui*. We are compelled, as viewers, to control our own bodies while we observe the ... yes ... the intuitive construction, but there are some things we cannot control ... the Other ...'

'Other people and their impatience, their schedule, their desire.'

'Hmm.' Hawi shrugs. 'But for me . . . I'm afraid that for me it's just too much of a dance. The work itself is naturalness . . . is beauty . . . but the *transaction* . . . I feel . . . I feel policed by the transaction.'

John Lincoln Braithwaite looks up from the iPad, 'You will not . . . uh . . . *se soumettre* . . . you refuse . . . *se refuser* to submit?'

'Uhhh . . .' Hawi ponders this statement. John Lincoln Braithwaite watches her, keenly, as she ponders.

'*Egotisme!*' he chuckles, 'And this is the genius of the work, surely? It evokes self-examination?'

'Not the work,' Hawi persists, 'The transaction.'

'The work *is* the transaction. Beauty comes at a price.'

Hawi thinks for a while, 'No. Beauty is free. I believe that. Also joy . . .' she grins, 'And I *am* able of stillness,' she insists, 'that is not the problem. Trust me – I am *too* able of stillness . . .'

'Really?' John Lincoln Braithwaite is charmed (in spite of himself) by her mispronunciation of 'capable', but he still looks sceptical, 'Is it possible to be *too* still?' he demands, 'Surely this work interrogates our *inability*, as a culture, to simply rest in things? *Repos*. To remain passive? To quietly receive?'

'Uhhh . . .' Hawi shakes her head, 'I am thinking quite the opposite. I would argue that our culture is *too* passive. We are glued to our phones. The algorithm choose *for* us. There is greater power in *mouvement*. In *résistance*. Although, *oui*, yes, of course, stillness *can* represent a kind of . . . of offering ... Hmm ...' she bursts out laughing, 'Passivity is complex, *non?*'

John Lincoln Braithwaite shrugs, 'It's precisely these conversations, these interrogations, that make the work so powerful. I see this as a meditation on sensuality – about the tug-of-war between power and desire.'

They both stare at the film.

'Um. I guess we all bring who we are to this space ... *nous-mêmes* ... and to the way that we process our *own* power, our *own* powerlessness. For me ...' Hawi winces, 'well ... for me ... as ... as *une femme* ... a woman ... and because I was ... uh ... a *religieuse* ...?'

John Lincoln Braithwaite scowls: 'A ...? Sorry?'

'A *religieuse* ...?'

He starts, 'A nun?'

'*Oui*. Nun.'

'You were a nun?'

'*Oui*.'

'Oh. Okay ... Wow.'

He is gazing at Hawi now, intrigued, 'How long since ...?'

'One year. I was a *religieuse* for 18 year.'

'You were a nun for *18 years*?'

'*Oui*.'

'Forgive me, Hawi, but how old are you?'

'I am 37 year.'

'You became a nun at ... at 18?'

'*Je l'ai fait*. Although I was in a ... um ... *couvent* from 16, and before then I was ...'

'Where? Here? In France?'

'Kenya.'

'And now you work as a Registrar? In a Parisian art gallery?' John Lincoln Braithwaite seems astonished by the sheer improbability of this journey.

'*Oui.* Emilien is my uncle – by marriage. He takes pity on me. The ex-nun . . .' Hawi laughs, '. . . and yes . . . so this mean that I have uh . . . a complex relation to passivity. In Catholicism we call this *obéissance* . . . yes? Obedience?'

'Okay. Right. Fair enough.'

They are both quiet for a while. Thinking. The film of the woman arranging her hair plays out in full.

Eventually Hawi says, 'I wear *blanc*. In Africa the *religieuse* wear white. I still cannot dress in colour. Colours are life. I am still . . . in some way . . . passive . . . attached . . .'
She sighs.

John Lincoln Braithwaite laughs wryly, 'And I actually thought . . .' he begins.

'What?' Hawi wonders, intrigued.

'Nothing.' He looks bashful.

'*What?!*' Hawi demands, chuckling, 'You found me pretentious? This black girl who wear only white?'

'I did!' he admits, '*Oui!* I'm afraid I did think that.'

'*Assez juste!*' Hawi pretends to be scandalised.

'*Je suis désolé*,' John Lincoln Braithwaite looks sincerely apologetic, 'I'm sorry.'

'Now you know who I am,' Hawi grins, 'This is me.'

'*Oui.* Thank you. I am . . . honoured . . . *honoré* . . .'

He dips his head a fraction, in obeisance, then adds 'The artwork uncovered you – it revealed you ... uh ... *mettre à nu* ...'

'Oh! *Que Dieu me preserve!*'

She blushes.

He gazes at her, rendered momentarily awkward by her awkwardness, but also delighted. 'Your sister is named after the season of the white ants ... *termite* ...' he recalls, 'What are you named after? Ha-wi?'

Hawi ponders this question for a moment, 'Okay,' she bargains, 'I will answer this question of yours if you will answer *my* question.'

'Hmm,' he looks wary, 'Okay.'

'Okay?'

John Lincoln Braithwaite nods.

'Okay. So my name is a Luo name – the Luo are my tribe. It means *bonne chance* ... good luck, or a blessing.'

'That's lovely.' John Lincoln Braithwaite smiles, 'Well you definitely got the better deal ...'

'*Pardon?*'

'Your sister drew the short straw ... uh ... *Termites*?'

'She did.' Hawi nods, gravely, '*Oui*. Angweng – *ma soeur* – was murder during the tribal clashes in Kenya in 1992 between the Luo and the Kikuyu. I often think ... uh ... *je réfléchis* ... she was name for destruction. I was name for salvation. There is much in ... in naming. I don't say this ... you know ... *banalement* ...'

'Tritely. You don't say that tritely,' John Lincoln Braithwaite

is appalled, 'No. I don't think you *could* say that tritely. I'm sorry, Hawi. Names are . . . yes . . . *important* . . .'
They watch the film in silence. The film feels almost painful to watch now.

'I am a little . . . *un petit peu* . . . uncomfortable,' John Lincoln Braithwaite finally admits, '. . . you know . . . all my . . . my preconceptions. You have unravelled them. I, too, have been uh . . . exposed . . . by this artwork.'

'Honestly. There is no need to feel this . . .' Hawi shakes her head, frowning, 'How could you be expected to know?'

When he sees Hawi frowning, John Lincoln Braithwaite realises that Hawi never frowns. Her face is . . . it is round and plump and almost . . . almost feels as if it has been solely constructed for light . . . for joy.
She *is* a blessing, he thinks. And for some reason he finds this thought almost unbearably painful.

Hawi is still talking, 'It was a long time ago,' she says, '*Il y a longtemps*. And I would not have raised it . . . just . . . you know . . . the *termite* . . .'

'Of course.'

'I cannot . . . uh . . . I cannot refuse the acknowledgement of my sister. This would feel . . . to deny her life . . . her spirit, *non?* Because I live . . . I live with this spirit. The truth of it, *pour toujours*. Always. This burns . . . *dans mon coeur* . . . right here . . .'
Hawi touches her heart. The film stops playing.

'The film stopped playing when you touched your . . .' John Lincoln Braithwaite looks down at his iPad, blinking.

One of the other Art Handlers yells something indecipherable from the far corner of the gallery.

The film commences playing from the beginning again.

John Lincoln Braithwaite looks up, 'You wanted to ask me a question, Hawi?'

Hawi grins, 'I do. *Oui*, I do want to ask you a question.'

'Okay. Then fire away.'

'Okay,' Hawi thinks for a moment, 'Uh . . .' she chuckles, 'Forgive me. I am nervous.'

'Really?' he frowns, '*Nerveuse? Pourquoi?*'

'Because I want to ask you something . . . uh . . . *un peu impertinent*, something about . . . uh . . .' she grimaces as she utters it: 'TonyInterruptor? *Oui?* This . . . this strange . . . "construct". I want to find out if you are aware . . . if you know . . . that this work is inspired by *your* interruption. This work originates with *you*, something *you* did. I just wonder . . . wondered . . . how that feels?'

John Lincoln Braithwaite watches the film in silence. He is frowning.

'Have I . . .' Hawi looks anxious, 'Did I *offend*?'

'Uh . . . No. You did not offend me, Hawi. But also – at the same time – I do not like to think about these things. I *éviter* . . . I avoid. Because it's uncomfortable. It makes me feel . . . um . . . unreal . . . *irréel*.'

'Ah!' Hawi covers her mouth with her hands, '*Je suis désolée*. I suspect it would be so!'

'Then why do you ask?' he wonders. He is not angry. He is interested.

'I ask because I had a conversation in London, at the show,' she explains, 'This show. At the opening. I had a conversation with one of the artist – Kinebuchi. It was a long conversation. I found her … delightful. She was delightful. And obviously … we see her in one of the artwork …' Hawi points to another part of the gallery, 'Arranging her hair.'

The film stops playing.

John Lincoln Braithwaite nods, '*Oui. Nous faisons.*'

'So she told me that this one act – this one gesture, of yours – this one gesture … uh … when you ask: Is this honest? *Est-ce honnête?* This gesture change everything for so many people involve. This one gesture – this interruption – the *conséquence* were so enormous for all people involve. And also for her own creative life. The two artists were *réunis* … they found each other, because of this interruption. And this gesture – your gesture – inform the artwork because … at the start it was just the women … the men … with their hair … the 'intuitive construction' … but then … uh … what you had done … they felt they need to interrupt the piece … because the … uh … ramification … *conséquences* … of what you did … were … they became about how *we* watch something … how *we* receive … and this was all … this was all you. *Vous tous.*'

There is a long silence.

'Wow. Okay … Uh … So the … the element of this work that you like *least* …?' he grins, 'That was me? The transaction? That was me?'

Hawi laughs. 'Haha. *Oui!* But my intention is not to cause

offence. It is more . . . I am fascinated by how this culture . . . it just . . . it *dévore* . . . it consume . . .'

'I see. Yes. I see that,' he confirms, 'I can see that.'

'So when I discover . . . I discover that *you* . . . you are handling this artwork, then my mind is like . . . *Boufff!*'

She mimes blowing her brains out with a handgun.

The film stops playing.

'I can see the . . . I can definitely see the . . . the irony,' John Lincoln Braithwaite concedes.

'Even now. Here,' Hawi continues on, excitedly, 'You are . . . you have got your iPad and you are trying to resolve . . . to police . . . the interruptions, which are only there because of what *you* did. And now . . . we see . . . you are the steward . . . the steward? Is this correct? You are the . . .'

'Yes. That's a great word. I am . . . I am here with the iPad and I am the . . . the "steward" . . .'

John Lincoln Braithwaite nods his head, wryly.

'It must be very strange . . .' Hawi smiles.

He nods. 'It's certainly pretty . . . pretty convoluted.'

'And now? Now I feel this . . . uh . . . guilt. Because maybe you didn't know? And now I make you . . . self-conscious?'

'I *didn't* know. You are right to think that. I *didn't* know . . . but I suspect that I also *did* know. I chose to be oblivious. I chose to remain . . . clean? Innocent? And now that I know . . . here . . .'

He points to his chest . . . 'it *is* a kind of . . . yes . . . a kind of . . . now you put it like that . . . a kind of . . .' he laughs, '. . . *agonie*.'

'*Oui*. Now I have *décrit* the *agonie* to you. I spell it out.'

Hawi winces.

'You have. You have spelled it out. And you have done this very ... very gently. Very kindly.'

'*Merci*.'

'And I can see why you found it interesting. Because ... well, it *is* interesting. It's ...'

'Once this interruption happen ... it is like ... like the problem in the machine ... the technical fault ... It repeats and it repeats. Interruption inspire interruption. Soon it is just ... urgh ... *bavardage*.'

'Just babble. Yes. Okay. This is very painful, and also very profound. And I am ... how to say this ... I am ...'

'*Pur*,' Hawi interrupts, 'You are pure. I see this. So to discuss this ... it is ... Because I was a nun. I can understand. These feelings. These battles. To stay ... *pur*. To stay ... in the body. To stay true. This is your *intégrité*.'

'It's almost ... it's almost impossible for me to contemplate ...'

'*Corruption*.'

'Yes. We exist inside our illusions.'

'*Exactement!* I was nun. I live inside these illusion more, perhaps, than anyone? They are beautiful illusion. And why not? Is what is real so much better than the illusion? Here I am, in my white. Dressing in my white. My illusion wear this white. I still cling to these illusion. They are *me*. They are ... yes ...' she grins, apologetically, 'ridiculous.'

'Ah. To be pure ...' John Lincoln Braithwaite shrugs, laughing.

'Our idealism is *pur* . . . but also fierce,' Hawi attempts to defend them both, 'It is not passive. It does not sit quietly during the performance . . . the prayer . . . it burns. It has the innocence . . . the fire . . . to destroy.'

'That's a terrifying thought,' John Lincoln Braithwaite admits.

'So I, Hawi, am this blessing,' Hawi rejoins, 'but also, a curse.'

'No.' John Lincoln Braithwaite shakes his head, emphatically, 'No. You are not a curse, Hawi. You are not a curse. You are . . . a revelation.'

'*Merci*. Do I believe you? Hmm.' Hawi chuckles.

'Revelations can be painful. The truth can be painful,' John Lincoln Braithwaite concedes.

'*Oui*. And I am at once sorry that I ask, but also . . . also . . . it's like this judgement was waiting for you. Because you offer this judgement . . . *aux autres*. For others. So it was waiting for you. In return. This is . . . *justice. No?* This is . . . *life. No?* What hurts? What is . . . *couleur*?'

Hawi gazes at him, her dark eyes glowing. John Lincoln Braithwaite feels eviscerated and blessed, all at once.

'Yes.' he says, finally. 'Yes. That is absolutely . . . *inéluctablement* . . . true.'

2

India Shore is standing in the stalls, three rows from the front, her back to the stage, aggressively scanning the audience. It is a medium-sized theatre and it is already half-full. People are milling around, inspecting their tickets and trying to find their seats. The faded velvet curtains on the stage (once a lustrous red, now an intriguing dusky pink) are drawn. The stage is set for a musical performance. It is opening night. There is an atmosphere – a buzz – of restrained excitement.

'I knew this was a mistake,' Lambert Shore murmurs to the back of the head of the stranger sitting in front of him.

'I knew this was a mistake,' he repeats.

India says nothing. She continues scanning.

'We had an agreement,' Lambert persists, 'You promised to be reasonable. You promised not to make a scene.'

'I *am* being reasonable!' India is indignant, 'I'm just . . . you know . . . trying to see if she's here.'

'This is *Fi's* night,' Lambert hisses, 'We are here to support Fi, remember?'

India says nothing.

'For all you know, she could be hiding in the very back rows of the circle, or curled up in the corner of one of the boxes. She could be somewhere backstage. In a dressing room, watching remotely. Or maybe she's not even here. Maybe she decided to stay in . . . I don't know . . . in Singapore . . .'

'Are you serious?' India is scornful, 'The album is called *Mallory Shore*, Dad. He named it *after* her. It's a "meditation on love". It's the opening night of the tour. *She's here.* How could she *not* be here?'

'Because Mallory is basically the Richey Edwards of Kent,' Lambert sighs, 'She does nothing by halves. And she's predictably unpredictable.'

'Richey who?'

'The guitarist with . . .'

'She has no reason to suspect we'd be here tonight,' India interrupts, 'It's hardly like . . .'

'Oh-*ho* she'd know all right,' Lambert snorts, 'This is *Mallory*, India. The two cornerstones of her character are her obsessive levels of attention to detail and her nascent paranoia. She'll know that this is the only live performance Fi has committed to in the past three years. She'll know that I would always move heaven and earth to support my . . .'

'Your . . .?'

India plops down into her seat, intrigued, 'Your . . .?'

'My friend. My collaborator.'

'Your collaborator?' India scoffs, 'Is it really so hard to admit that you and Fi are a couple now? To yourself? To each other?'

Lambert looks horrified; 'You conveniently forget that Fi has . . .'

'Oh come *on*. Larry lives in Berlin. They see each other, at best, four times a year. Mallory has gone – *pouf* – disappeared. Fi's been effectively *living in our home* since I started college.'

Lambert grimaces and glances around him, discomforted, 'I hate to burst this lovely, romantic bubble of yours,' he mutters, 'but Fi and I have been focusing all our energy on creating art together. We've been . . .'

'Yes, yes, *yes*,' India groans, 'You've been . . . a-*hem*. "Constructing Intuitively" . . .'

(Lambert had actually been intending to say 'rather busy').

'Although she's been a great support with Gunn,' Lambert ploughs on, 'ever since . . . well . . .'

'Urgh.'

India throws back her head, despairing, and gazes up at the tastefully gilded ceiling. She grabs her phone from her pocket, taps Camera, and takes a picture.

'D'you think Mallory might be planning to make a surprise appearance, mid-set?' Lambert ponders, drolly, 'Perhaps swinging onto the stage from a chandelier?'

India refuses to bite. She straightens back up again.

'Why won't everyone . . . *you* . . . *Fi* . . . just . . . just be open about what is *actually* happening here?' she demands, 'Engage with the true … true *substance* of the thing? Stop framing everything in terms of ART and IDEAS and MEANING, stop communicating only in GESTURES and SYMBOLS, stop always making everything so … so INTELLECTUAL, so META, and just … just … for once in your life risk being *real*?'

'Meta?' Lambert echoes, bemused, 'What does that even mean? Cerebral? Considered? *Rational?*'

India sighs.

Yup. Okay. Here we go …

'Anyway, isn't "real" a relative concept?' Lambert argues, 'Are your "real" and my "real" even remotely comparable? Perhaps if I started filming everything on my iPhone and posting endlessly self-referential content into cyberspace … if I stopped quietly subsisting – like some soulless husk – inside the rarified ART bubble … Maybe, *then*, by your standards, I might be considered "real"?'

India rolls her eyes at what is, she instantly deduces, a perfect example of her dad's absolute determination to evade and obfuscate.

'Seriously, though, what *is* "real"?' Lambert persists, 'Are those two bouncers real?'

He points to the two shaven-headed, beefy and unsmiling men who have recently walked to the front of the auditorium and are now standing, facing the audience, scowling, on either side of the stage. 'The trolls, the hecklers, are they real? And Fi's stage fright … three years of stage fright. "Real"? "Unreal"? The online abuse? The stalker? Were they "real"? Were the threats "real threats"? Okay. Yes. This has all – for the most part – unfolded online . . . remotely . . . digitally . . . But Fi's responses have been . . . *are* . . . very "real".'

'Please don't try to make out that I'm trivialising what Fi has been through . . .' India effortlessly matches, then raises, Lambert's high levels of indignation.

'It's just . . .' Lambert ponders, 'You're nineteen years old and full of all of this adorable rigour and innocence and idealism, and I *love* that about you, but still . . . I mean . . . the sheer . . . the unbelievable *arrogance* . . .'

'Are you scared of losing the moral high ground?' India deftly counters, 'Is that it?'

'Sorry?' Lambert's head jerks around.

'Or perhaps you're terrified of commitment?' India speculates, 'And who could blame you? I mean after Mum got her PPL, went commercial, fell in love with her chief purser and buggered off to God-knows-where-next?'

'Uh . . .' Lambert is briefly thrown off his stride by the unexpected sophistication of his daughter's attack.

'Then Mallory just . . . well . . . *evaporating*?' India continues to expand her train of thought. She glances over at him, expectantly.

'Do we actually . . .?' Lambert is unable to understand why India feels compelled to rehash all of this stuff *right now* (here, in public) when countless other careful attempts on his part to engage her on these issues (and in private) have failed.

'Although – to be fair,' India concedes, 'Mum still questions the timeline around her first long-hauls for Virgin and you "offering support" to your favourite student . . .'

'Mallory majored in *law*,' Lambert is outraged (and this outrage is surely a convenient vehicle on which to mount a swift escape from his daughter's psychological headlock), 'She never studied architecture.' He glares at her, accusingly, 'And she was a mature student when we met. An adult. She wasn't my "favourite student". She wasn't even *my* student. She just sat in on one of my lectures while waiting for a ride home during an industrial . . .'

They both stand up to allow a couple of people to squeeze past and find their seats.

'D'you still think she might just show up one of these days?' India wonders (they are sitting down again now).

'Sorry?'

Lambert is rearranging his jacket on his lap.

'*Mallory*.'

'Show up?' he scowls.

'Yeah. That she might just turn up at the house? Let herself in with her keys? You'll find her sitting at the kitchen table with a large fruit cake. And she'll say, "I just really want to apologise for walking out on you and India AND MY CHILD – *her* child! – with no explanation whatsoever . . ."' Lambert shakes his head, 'For the record, um, no. I don't think . . .'

'I mean I can't imagine there'll be a song in Sasha Keyes's set tonight focusing on *that* charming little detail, do you?'

Lambert pretends to consider this question seriously, and then . . . 'I don't expect there will be, no. But for the record, it's *my* name on Gunn's birth certificate. I watched her draw her first breath. I cut the cord. I am her father not by necessity, biology or by accident but by *choice*. I chose her. Gunn is *my* child, much as that idea now seems to baffle and astonish you . . .'

The softness of Lambert's voice both expresses and belies his hurt. Isn't it bad enough that he feels compelled (although there was no pressure from Fi – not so much as an *ounce* of it) to attend the premiere of an album – a meditation *on love* – named after his estranged wife? And now India being so . . . um . . . undilutedly and persistently . . . well . . . 'India'?

'No wonder it was always so tense . . . so . . . so stressy in that house,' India grumbles (obviously remarking, internally, on her father's slight change in tone), 'Nothing ever really *sat* right. I had this . . . this *feeling*, this *intuition* . . . but I kept trying to ignore it. I always *knew*, at some level, that Gunn wasn't . . .'

'If you could just . . .'

Lambert makes a 'bring it down' gesture with his hands, like a conductor quietening an unruly horn section.

'It's like I was standing on a beach, staring out at the ocean,' India describes – nay *illustrates* – this scene with both of her hands, 'and there's this giant . . . this monumental ICEBERG blocking out the horizon. I'm looking at it, pointing at it, kind of dumbstruck and scared . . . I'm just a kid – I don't even have the *language* yet . . .' she gazes at him, poignantly, 'but then you and Mallory . . . you and Mallory just keep on turning me away, steering me towards the dunes, handing me my little plastic bucket and spade and telling me to build *sand*castles . . .'

Lambert takes off his glasses and pinches the skin at the top of his nose. His eyes feel dry.

'Might you be hamming things up just a little . . .?' he wonders.

'Shocking, isn't it?' India laughs, bitterly, 'That I should dare to have *actual feelings* around this stuff?'

They both stand up again as another couple squeezes past.

'But was it even really a lie?' Lambert wonders, sitting down again, '. . . because we honestly . . . we simply . . . uh . . . didn't think . . . we just presumed . . .?'

'Hmm. I suspect there's an official term for that.'

India lifts up her phone and googles. Lambert waits patiently (even though he knows, full well, how this will turn out). As she focuses on the screen India murmurs, 'I mean for two of the most opinionated people *on earth* to somehow, miraculously, forget to . . .'

She deftly adjusts her search description, scowling, 'If it wasn't for that blood drive at school . . . if I hadn't actually . . .' then, 'Omission!' she whoops, triumphant, 'A lie by omission!'

She points to her screen and reads out loud: '"The theology behind a sin of omission derives from *James 4:17* which teaches: 'Anyone, then, who knows the right thing to do and fails to do it, commits sin.'"'

SIN

Oh Lord.

Lambert glances up towards the stage (a slight air of desperation) then down at his watch. Shouldn't they have started playing *five minutes* ago?

Sin?

Is that even a word – a concept – that anyone takes seriously nowadays?

India runs her finger down the page and deftly presses the *People Also Ask* link: *Is a lie of omission still a lie?* The link instantly unfurls and again, she reads:

'"All in all, omission can be just as, if not more, damaging than lying, as it manipulates a person's perception of what's real and what's not. By undermining trust in interpersonal relationships, lying by omission is a *recipe for disaster*."'

Lambert is now, officially, a small moth (nothing fancy. Not a Death's-head Hawkmoth or a bright green Luna Moth, or a Tiger Moth or an Atlas Moth. No. None of these. Just a small, dusty Clothes Moth or a humble, rug-munching Carpet Moth) which has been efficiently gassed, identified, labelled, and pinned onto a board – a giant panel. Or perhaps he has been set into a block of clear acrylic? Like a paperweight? Yes. He is a common-or-garden Carpet Moth trapped inside a clear acrylic paperweight. India rests the paperweight – rests *him* – in her palm. She can place him wheresoever she damn well chooses, and she knows it.

'Well I think that's all fairly definitive,' she smirks, glancing up.

'Maybe *this*,' he mutters, tight-lipped, 'is why we generally chose to avoid the subject?'

India's jubilation at the success of her Google search instantly evaporates.

'This?' she echoes, '*This?!* What exactly are we talking about here, Dad? My completely valid and legitimate feelings of *hurt* and *sense of betrayal*?'

Lambert winces. Okay. It's official. He really is a dick.

'Surely "*this*" is precisely why you should've told me?' she continues, 'I had a right to know that the person being raised as my biological sister was not, in fact, my biological sister. God! That house was . . . it still is, *creaking* with . . . with . . .'

Bottom line? India loves her dad. Perhaps he *is* just a common-or-garden Clothes Moth or a Carpet Moth (slightly maddening, destructive, pesky). Even so. She has no desire to swat him, to wound him, to crush or to exterminate him. She only wants to poke an inquisitive digit at him, provoke him a little, make him flutter around in panic and scatter a bit of wing-dust. That's all. Because hasn't he been punished enough? Didn't her mum leave and then Mallory just . . . *pouf!*? Isn't he in sole care of a child with special needs who is not even *his*, biologically? Aren't they waiting for the opening performance of a meditation on love named after his ex?

'. . . with . . . with *humbug*!' she finally settles.

Humbug?

'"Humbug"?!' Lambert echoes, laughing (relieved), 'But surely your main problem with Mallory was her complete *lack* of humbug? You loathed her brashness, her brutal . . . almost ruthless honesty.'

'Brash, yes,' India concedes, 'Brutal, definitely. But honest, Dad? *Honest?!*'

'. . . And Mallory's main problem with *you*,' Lambert completes his point, nonetheless (and is deeply struck by the irony of it), 'was your absolute determination to always speak your mind and damn the consequences . . .'

'We were like two flies pointlessly arguing over a freeze-dried mouse dropping,' India mutters, 'while casually hovering in front of a steaming muck heap.'

'Have you ever considered swapping Graphic Design for Creative Writing?' Lambert wonders. He is perfectly serious. 'Although . . .' he gazes at his daughter, almost admiring, 'What could they possibly hope to teach you?'

'All the stuff with her hair,' India ignores him, 'I *sensed* it was about something more than simply . . . you know . . . just a "look". I *sensed* it was a kind of . . . like in gambling, in poker . . . a *tell* . . .'

'Okay.'

Two well-dressed but slightly tipsy women are settling into their seats just to the left of him. Lambert lowers his voice still further, 'Much as it would delight me to be able to neatly reduce this challenging, sad, messed-up, painful, *nuanced* situation into the neat binary of right and wrong, maybe even end it – or heal it – with a quick and easy apology, I can't. It's impossible to.'

'I'm not looking for an apology,' India snorts, 'I just want you to admit that a truth is felt. It just . . . it just *is*. And I knew,' she lifts a hand to her chest, 'I just *knew*.'

For some reason, this small hand-on-heart gesture infuriates her father.

Does *his* lived experience amount to nothing, then? *His* 'knowing'? All that unexpressed and inexpressible confusion – compromise – endurance that is part and parcel of any relationship, but especially that of parenthood? Because weren't her – and Gunn's – *feelings* the main reason why he always felt compelled to hold back? To bite his tongue? If only in the hope of shielding them? Of sheltering them?

'No! *No*,' he snaps, 'You *didn't* know. You just like to *think* that you knew because it gives you a satisfying feeling of moral superiority.'

One of the women to the left of Lambert belches loudly then says, 'Oops!' and giggles. Lambert ignores her.

'. . . Anyway, simply "feeling" something doesn't automatically make it right or true,' he continues, 'People "feel" stupid things all the time. I "feel" like I would've been an amazing drummer, even though I have no natural sense of rhythm . . .' he looks to his daughter for confirmation, and, against her better judgement, she grins.

'This is the limbic brain, the "lizard brain", in action,' he continues, 'Its responses are powerful but primitive. Fight or flight. Freeze or fawn . . . possibly . . .' he shrugs, apologetically, 'fornication. All the Fs. It's the thing that makes us fearful of strangers. Or afraid of the dark. Or suspicious of avocados . . .'

(Shore Family Lore records that India had been deeply suspicious of avocados right up until the very moment that they became her favourite food.)

Urgh. India scowls. What?! The avocado thing, *again*?

'Gut feelings can't always be the ultimate test of right or wrong . . .' Lambert is delighted to observe how hard the avocado detail hits . . . 'Integrity, justice, all the good stuff . . . it's measured, it's calculated and very occasionally it's counter-intuitive. It's difficult, India. It's contested. It's *hard*.'

'Oh. Okay,' India hisses straight back, 'So my deeply felt intuition, my powerful gut response is automatically "lizard brain" now? Thanks for gaslighting me, Dad!'

Lambert chooses not to rise to this (because surely she has a point?).

'It was messy,' he sighs, 'And I'm really sorry about that. But Mal . . .' he stops, and peers around him, cautiously, 'M was weighed down by a lot of self-loathing and guilt. She grew up in the care system, separated from her brother, being shunted from foster placement to foster placement. There was no security, no . . .'

'Yes, yes,' India interrupts, her voice hardening, 'Poor old Mallory. Let's make *constant* excuses for poor old Mallory, because of all the terrible stuff she went through as a kid . . .'

'She was fresh out of rehab when we first became friends,' Lambert persists (he must just keep on telling the story, because only the story brings him relief . . . brings him clarity), 'She showed up, randomly, at a couple of my classes. She was always original . . . challenging, inquisitive . . .' he grimaces, 'She had no idea she was pregnant and then no clue who the father was. She was scared but she was brave,' he shrugs, 'And she knew – even then – that the consequences of so much self-abuse and neglect for the foetus were not . . .'

'Ah . . . and look!' India sighs, 'Here comes Sir Galahad: clippety-clop-clippety-clop . . .'

'Well, I choose not to find myself ridiculous,' Lambert snaps, 'At the time it felt right and it felt good and it felt . . . I don't know . . . generous. It felt . . . "*real*".'

'Huh.' India sucks on her tongue and glances over her shoulder again, at the rapidly filling theatre.

'And the hair thing was just . . . just sad,' he continues, somewhat haltingly, 'She had beautiful hair. This wild, dark halo of hair which she'd spent most of her life peeking through or hiding behind. Maybe she felt like she needed to punish herself after Gunn was born and shaved it off in some kind of penance? I don't know. Perhaps she wanted to force herself to be fully present, and by being present to stay sober. Which she did. No more hiding. For the best part of a decade.'

'Punish herself?!' India scoffs, 'She punished *all* of us by being a disgustingly meticulous and controlling cow.'

'She could be sharp,' Lambert shrugs, 'but she was very funny. And she was fully capable of laughing at herself . . .' he glances sideways at his daughter, 'You never really got the joke. You declared war on her from the outset because she wasn't – and would never be – your mum. But that was hardly her fault.'

'No!' India's hand clutches her phone, 'That wasn't it *at all*. You both lied to me about . . .'

Lambert shushes her, 'We didn't lie, we just didn't make explicit something that seemed obvious or . . . or irrelevant. Gunn was your sister because you wanted her to be, in the same way that she is my daughter because I wanted that, too. Secrets are the things that you keep hidden because you're *ashamed* of them. The point you keep missing is that I felt *no shame*. None.'

'I love Gunn,' India nods, 'You know that. And *you* love Gunn. Even *Fi* loves Gunn. But where's Mallory? Where's her mum?'

India stands up, as if thereby seeking to answer her own question. She turns, and begins peering around the auditorium again.

'Mallory was . . . *is* passionate,' Lambert sighs, 'and slightly obsessive – which is possibly something else the two of you have in common . . .' He rubs his forehead, suddenly drained, 'She loved Gunn deeply. But maybe it was too deep – too hard . . . too unrelenting? And was all that suppressed guilt and control good for Gunn in the long run? Probably not. Mallory couldn't change who she was, what she'd done, how she felt . . .'

'Hmm,' India shoves her fringe out of her eyes, 'I don't know. I don't know about that. To say a person just can't love right . . . that they can't learn to love better? That the answer isn't to just *loosen the fuck up*? That it's healthier to simply walk out? To bugger off? To find someone you can love more easily? Do that instead? Erase the past? Erase the people in it? That's ridiculous. It's cowardly. It's messed up.'

'I'm struggling to understand why you're so angry about her leaving when you strongly resented her being there in the first place,' Lambert rejoins, 'You can't have your cake and eat it. Anyway . . .' he shakes his head. 'She didn't *decide*. It wasn't "thought out". She suffered a psychotic episode after a reaction to pain meds. Something . . . something shifted. It wasn't rational. It certainly wasn't premeditated. But maybe – just maybe – it was ultimately for the greater good.'

'Dad. News Flash!' India isn't buying it, 'She never came home from the hospital. She never came home. *She never came home*. It's been three years! And now, here we are, sitting in a London theatre, awaiting the live performance of an album named after her by *Sasha Keyes*, who just happens to be this season's Sir Galahad. It is crazy. It is crazy. It's crazy.'

'Not sitting,' Lambert corrects her, 'Standing. You are *standing* in the theatre and making a complete spectacle out of us both.'

The auditorium is now almost full. Several musicians have wandered out onto the stage and are tuning their instruments. India doesn't want to sit down, but she sits down.

'I mean where does the buck stop?' Lambert wonders, as much to himself as to his daughter; 'Does the buck *ever* really stop? If we hadn't attended the gig that night, if TonyInterruptor hadn't spoken up, if you hadn't accidentally filmed it . . .'

As he speaks, the lights go down in the auditorium. The lights go up on the stage. Sasha Keyes walks into view holding his muted trumpet (to a brief, yet appreciative, round of applause). He looks different. More relaxed. His hair is longer and tucked behind his ears. No jacket or tie, just a bone-coloured T-shirt, loose jeans and black trainers. He seems vulnerable, but somehow ... uncluttered. He seems *clean*.

From the other side of the stage, Fi appears. She too looks different. She is wearing a bright, loosely cut red smock over a wide, long, loudly patterned dress with a pair of baggy orange trousers peeking out underneath. She is a symphony of contrasting layers above bright green trainers. Most of this outfit (Lambert knows) was acquired with him (under his tutelage) on a recent trip to China to discuss the commission of a piece of sculpture/sound art for the Shanghai Sculpture Park. She seems confident and stylish. Her hair is gathered up into a topknot. Her lips are highlighted by a sharp smear of lipstick.

Several people clap (Lambert among them). Someone makes an inexplicable parp-ing sound. A few people look around, bemused. The audience quietens.

'Oh. Okay. So now *I'm* suddenly responsible for this whole surreal car-crash?' India mutters, 'Now it's partly *my* fault?'

Sasha nods to the crowd then signals to Tod Knowles on drums. He leans against a stool. Tod starts to play, with his brushes, very softly, and is soon joined by a bluesy piano (Simo Treen is notable tonight by his absence). Fi picks up her guitar but simply rests it on her thigh.

'No. *No.* That's precisely my point,' Lambert whispers back, 'It's not about blame. No one is at fault. We're all just trying to stagger our way through this shitstorm with some tiny shreds of dignity still intact.'

A person behind shushes him.

They both gaze up at the stage. The music is very spare but extremely tender and beautiful. A little bit Erik Satie, a subtle hint of Debussy. Soft, sensual, soulful . . .

'And so, *once again*,' India mutters, 'Mallory slithers effortlessly off the hook . . .'

Ten-second pause.

'Nobody is slithering *anywhere*,' Lambert hisses back, 'Have a heart. You don't think she suffered enough? You don't think, at some level, that she's *still* suffering?'

Another *shush* from behind. Lambert scowls.

'Surely you re-invent yourself to *avoid* suffering,' India murmurs.

On stage, Sasha Keyes lifts up his muted trumpet and begins to play. The effortlessly powerful, almost keening sound he produces reminds Lambert, from the very first blow, of Miles, resplendent, on *Blue in Green*. It is authoritative yet vulnerable. It is jagged. It is exquisitely tender.

Lambert's eyes fill with tears.

Wow.

He blinks. This is absolutely . . . this is absolutely, fucking *unbearable!*

What a fool!

How had he not realised?

That this would be absolutely, fucking unbearable?

His throat tightens. His instinct is to either jump up and leave, or to remain seated, hunch over and bawl. But he can do neither. Instead he turns to his daughter and says; 'People are never just *one thing*, India. Good or bad, true or false. We're all flawed, all beautiful, all riddled with . . .'

'Excuse me.'

A small torch is being shone directly at Lambert from the aisle. He finds himself spotlit. It is an usher. The usher places a warning finger to his lips, and then, in two further, neat gestures, silently informs Lambert that he is in danger of being evicted from the theatre. The torch goes off. He withdraws.

Lambert is embarrassed. India murmurs something, but it is so quiet that at first he thinks she is merely offering a few gentle words of consolation. He is wrong. Her words are anything but conciliatory. Even so, it takes him a moment to decipher.

'Isn't it odd that Mallory left on the *very day* she found out about the Intuitive Constructions project . . .?'

Just to be sure, he repeats this sentence, softly, in his head.

'Isn't it odd that Mallory left on the *very day* she found out about the Intuitive Constructions project?'

Lambert scowls, '*What?!*'

He enunciates – like a stroke victim – from one side of his mouth.

But . . . but . . . but . . . didn't she realise? Hadn't he told her – *and* Mallory – at the time? It wasn't *real* . . . none of it . . . not at first. It was all just a ruse, an act, a sham . . .

He can't speak. And India remains blissfully oblivious, since she is now, rather conveniently, fully engrossed in the performance.

Up on stage, Sasha is just completing an evocative solo with an uncharacteristically theatrical flourish. He steps back, smiling (an appreciative smattering of applause), and leans against his stool, encouraging the other players to step into focus.

In that moment, Lambert briefly recalls a slightly awkward conversation between himself and Fi after the first full day of rehearsals for the album. It was only a week before recording, and Fi had just arrived home, patently frustrated by what she insisted was a complete turnaround – a dramatic upheaval – in Sasha's creative *modus operandi*.

Prior to this record, Sasha had always maintained a rigorously collective approach to composing. His motivation, as Fi understood it, was part-post-punk, part-leftist-ideology, part-natural-bellicosity. He'd always presented himself as a jazz militant, a theoretical zealot and a radical. For this reason, his traditional template (although Sasha was inherently allergic to the straitjackets of tradition and of templates) was to send each of his carefully selected cadre of players a memory stick (a few weeks prior to the recording date) on which he'd describe a particular mood, outline a basic theme, and possibly suggest a couple of loose chord progressions as an informal starting point. When the group finally assembled in person, for rehearsals, they'd brainstorm and exchange ideas, thwacking them vigorously back and forth until something landed. Sasha could be exacting and brutal during these relentless sallies (honest to a fault), but invariably receptive and responsive.

Fi often thought of starlings: a Murmuration of Starlings: the way they spontaneously traced the evening sky with a succession of dazzlingly fluid and ornate patterns. One bird initially led the way, then hundreds, maybe thousands more would casually fall into sync. At any given moment, though, if another bird was sufficiently emboldened, driven, or charismatic, then they, in their turn, could inspire a sudden and dramatic change of course, on the slightest – the merest – flap of a wing. Some might call this 'flow': the effortless melding together of action and consciousness; a special form of communion; a wordless rapport; a profound fellowship, a feeling of just . . . well, transcendent harmony.

That, in brief, was jazz improvisation. And this was the genius of Sasha Keyes: to be open; to make space for others to step forward, while still, by sheer force of will, leading.

Mallory Shore, though? This album? It was different. For starters, the score had been entirely composed and notated by Sasha, in advance. Before studio dates had even been finalised, the selected players had been sent their individual parts in a sound file and instructed to commit them to heart. Copious notes and suggestions were provided around mood and technique. Deviation was discouraged. Sasha now required – no, demanded – absolute fidelity. The notated score became walls and roof, Sasha stood guard at the door, and the players were expected to obediently occupy this strange, new sonic cell of his.

Fi naturally found this jarring. Surely in jazz, the freer you were, the truer and purer your practice? Was Sasha even *remotely penitent* for locking them all up in his aural penitentiary? For this blatant philosophical *volte-face*? Not a bit of it!

It felt like he'd lost his compulsion to endlessly riff on his subject. To worry away at it. To strive to be that one, dominant voice amid the cacophony of other voices – other ideas. Now there was certainty. Everything on *Mallory Shore*, the album, was micro-managed and definitive. It was unapologetically *his*.

As the rehearsals evolved, and they really began to play together, in earnest, Fi couldn't help but be moved by the music's joyful simplicity and effortless ebullience. It was serene and it was roomy and it spoke to a whole new sense of confidence and assurance on the part of its composer.

'I wonder,' she'd said, haltingly, 'if his relationship with . . . you know . . . Mallory . . .' she'd winced slightly on uttering her name, 'has forced . . . I mean *allowed* him to enter a whole new phase, musically? In the same way that *our* relationship . . .' she'd glanced over at Lambert, anxiously, 'It's like . . . we're still fundamentally the same people, but it's a whole new kind of . . . of discipline . . . of exchange . . .' she'd frowned, struggling to find a concise way of expressing it. 'Previously it was like Sasha's music – the spontaneous chemistry in the studio or on stage – was the unstable element. Uncertainty was freedom. But now . . . now it's like the music needs to be definitive because . . .' she'd tried, then failed, to utter Mallory's name for a second time, 'because *love* is so unstable. The music needs to feel safe, feel certain. *Love* has become the unstable element . . .'

She'd frowned for a moment, struggling to make her ideas cohere.

'And while a part of me feels frustrated by the change . . . or sad, I don't know, at the loss of my . . .' she'd shrugged, 'my sense of . . . of creative liberty, another part feels like there's a message in it . . . a lesson . . . for me, for all of us . . . because of the way that this new dynamic . . . this new kind of discipline . . . allows us to experience a different kind of freedom which is in *not* choosing . . . *not* deciding, even as we continue to vibrate against each other . . . move . . . reflex . . . react . . .'

A short silence followed. Lambert had – for the first time in his life, possibly – contributed absolutely nothing to the discussion.

'Or maybe it's just living and teaching in Osaka?' she'd finished up, flatly.

Ah, Mallory.
Mallory Shore.

After the initial panic and confusion of her leaving, a strange calm, then a million questions (but he'd asked none). Instead Lambert waited. He waited for her to return. And in the waiting . . . in the waiting . . . a kind of marvellous, clammy, prickling resignation. The waiting was like a large mosquito bite that, for some unsayable, unthinkable reason, he would not, *could* not scratch.

Perhaps this was the very point that Fi had been struggling to make? About the freedom of no freedom?

He'd certainly thought about the waiting a lot (in the same way he thought about everything), and he'd used some of the ideas he developed in his and Fi's first artwork. So wasn't all that keen analysis at the very least . . . constructive?

Then one day he finally realised, with a sense of palpable relief, that, to all intents and purposes, his *entire life* had consisted in waiting. It wasn't only this particular part of it. This part of it merely served to emphasise all the other parts . . . the other ways that he – that possibly everyone – waited. Waited for results. Waited for love. Waited for certainty. Waited for happiness. Waited for peace. Waited for arrival. Waited for judgement or belonging or resolution. He asked himself if this 'waiting mentality' was a specifically English mindset. Like queuing? Like standing boredly in line, but for ACTUAL LIFE? Just waiting for it to quietly make sense, then to finally start up, be officially unleashed, in earnest?

Occasionally something would happen (an accident, an illness, a birth, a betrayal) and the waiting would end. There would be . . . what to call it? A temporary *denouement*? A hiatus? But then the waiting would start up again shortly after. Just on another page. Within different parameters.

*

When Mallory left, he waited. It actually became a form of devotion. A presence in absence. It became the infinite possibility of an unanswered question.

Then, after seven months and three days, an email arrived, which read:

Lambert,
Have you ever heard of the Lineage of Mis-steps?
If you were seeking enlightenment, say, and you thought that you had to make all the right choices, do all the right things, just to reach it? Like the narrow path which Jesus talks about? You have to stay on it. All those rules. It's so very narrow and so very easy to fall off. Then everything is lost, of course. Ruined. Destroyed. And when you fall off the narrow path you descend into . . . where? Into Hell? Which is just . . .
Well, there are CONSEQUENCES.

But what if one day, quite out of the blue, you discovered a philosophy in which the mis-steps are actually the whole point? The mis-steps are a fundamental part of how you learn and grow? You are . . . I don't know . . . sanctified by all of those bad decisions? Your strength – your divinity – is the little, sweet nut hidden inside the hard shell of the disaster?

We both know that I have taken more than my fair share of mis-steps in my life. And now . . . well. Another huge one. But this time it feels different because I am trusting that the pain of it . . . the chaos . . . will take me exactly where I need to go. Just think: if mis-steps are the actual route . . . then maybe the legion of ways in which I have always messed up are suddenly . . . they brought me HERE, didn't they? And maybe this is where I always needed to be? And maybe it's not so terrible, after all?

And maybe . . . maybe when you decided to marry me, this, too, was a mis-step? And what is happening now is the lesson – the revelation – a message from the universe?

I cannot say I am sorry, Lambert. If I say that I am sorry then it means that I don't believe in the philosophy, and right now, the philosophy is the only thing I've got.

Forgive me.

I am not sorry.

Mallory

After two weeks of furious cogitation, his response:

Our love? Our family? A mis-step?

Mallory?

Their differences were surely irreconcilable.

Fi, with her freedom in no-freedom.
India with her deeply felt truths.
Mallory with her mis-steps.

For some reason, whenever he thinks of Mallory now, a song by Will Oldham plays in his head. It's called 'I Am a Cinematographer' and it is a small, plain, beautifully artless folk song. But the way Oldham sings the actual word, 'cinematographer', the way the rhythm seems to hang on it, allows the meaning to quietly shift from 'cine' to 'sinner'. I am a sinner-matographer. So Lambert inhabits *both* spaces as he hums. And he finds this deeply evocative; the way Oldham contains both the idea of sinning, and the notion of simply watching – waiting – and recording something: with cameras and with lights.

He isn't stupid. It's perfectly natural that sometimes he might wonder whether endlessly analysing this stuff (pausing to *think*, accepting the *wait*) is just his way of avoiding all those dark feelings of betrayal and rage, exhaustion and disappointment. Then at other times he feels like a cinematographer who is calmly lighting and recording his own life.

A talented professional.

Lambert is lost in these – and other – thoughts, when suddenly, and in real life, someone sitting at the far side of the stalls hurls an egg towards the stage. Then there is yelling. The content of the yelling is hard to decipher. Lambert is caught by surprise. He tunes in too late.

What?!

It seems like the egg has been aimed at Fi, but as it arcs towards her it hits the back of an amplifier and shatters. Fi had told him that she was ready for this. She was resigned to it. She knew that it would happen. Because people were very invested in something – a complex dynamic – between her and Sasha, and the *actual truth* of the thing (was there really even an actual truth? Wasn't it just a curious jangle of competing perspectives?) didn't seem to matter. It was irrelevant. The personalities – the exchange – the moment. All irrelevant. So trouble was to be expected. And she insisted that she was strong enough to handle it. Because she believed in this music. And she needed Lambert to know that and to be okay with it.

One of the bouncers leaps into the audience.

Then the drunk woman next to Lambert starts laughing, raucously. Perhaps it's just the shock of it, or maybe this was the exact reason she bought her ticket? Or maybe it isn't connected to the egg, or to Fi, or to . . . it's just . . .?

Lambert turns and says, 'Why don't you *SHUT THE FUCK UP*?'

(Oops. Did that come out a little louder than he'd intended?)

He glances towards the stage again. The musicians have stalled – are in disarray – for just a brief moment, but then Sasha calmly steps forward and turns to face them, he lifts his hand, and they gather themselves together and resume playing, with, if possible, even greater levels of resolution. The tenderness of the music feels like a kind of triumph, like a victory, like a brilliantly incongruous – even comical – soundtrack to the thrashing and the chaos now exploding in front of them.

Oh how apt, Lambert thinks, wryly.

India is standing up and filming. A small fight has erupted and Lambert is just pondering the manifold outcomes – for Fi, for the performance, for India – when he feels a heavy pressure on his shoulder. Hang on . . .?

Is it the laughing woman again, damn her?

Is it . . .?

He finds himself being dragged, in a necklock, from his seat, out into the aisle, towards the exit. He is halfway there before he realises that it is him. *He* is the unstable element. *He* is being evicted. It is *him*. Like an out-of-body experience. Utterly bizarre. And he can't fully comprehend why. He is yelling, 'You don't understand! I'm with the band! I am here to support Fi.' Then he is yelling, 'My daughter. I can't just leave without . . .'

As quickly as it begins, it is over. He is outside, in the street, patting off the dust from his knees. The door slams behind him. It is all so marvellously undignified. It is also very quiet and dark here. Definitive. Final. One of his ears has been pushed forward in the scuffle and is stinging a little. His heart is pumping. His cheeks are flushed.

He catches his breath for a second. He is astonished. He tries to gather himself together. He begins to walk – urgently, at speed – around the perimeter of the building, to try and find the front entrance in case India has left her seat to run after him.

*

It is then – now – that he sees her. Mallory. She is perched on a low wall, opposite the venue, smoking. Next to her: a stroller. A small child strapped into it. Mallory's hair has grown. This is his first thought. Then: is she heavily pregnant? Good God.
Smoking?!

I am a sinner-matographer.
Mallory glances up. *Oh shit.* Her face falls. She drops her cigarette.

Lambert stands still. He inhales. He nods. Then, with perfectly astonishing levels of care and exactitude, he quietly considers the quality of the lighting and calmly frames his shot.

ABOUT THE AUTHOR

NICOLA BARKER is the author of thirteen previous novels – including *Wide Open*, *Darkmans*, *The Yips* and *H(a)ppy* – and two short story collections. She has twice been longlisted and once shortlisted for the Booker Prize, longlisted for the Women's Prize for Fiction, has won the IMPAC Prize, the John Llewellyn Rhys Prize, the Hawthornden Prize and the Goldsmiths Prize, and was named one of *Granta*'s Best of Young British Novelists in 2003. She was born in Ely and lives in Kent.